Reincarnated as a sword

12

written by
Yuu Tanaka

illustrated by
Llo

Seven Seas Entertainment

Tensei Shitara Ken Deshita Vol. 12
©Yuu Tanaka (Story) ©Llo (Illustration)
This edition originally published in Japan in 2021 by
MICRO MAGAZINE, INC., Tokyo.
English translation rights arranged with
MICRO MAGAZINE, INC., Tokyo.

No portion of this book may be reproduced or transmitted
in any form without written permission from the copyright
holders. This is a work of fiction. Names, characters, places,
and incidents are the products of the author's imagination
or are used fictitiously. Any resemblance to actual events,
locales, or persons, living or dead, is entirely coincidental.
Any information or opinions expressed by the creators of this
book belong to those individual creators and do not necessarily
reflect the views of Seven Seas Entertainment or its employees.

Seven Seas press and purchase enquiries can be sent to
Marketing Manager Lianne Sentar at press@gomanga.com.
Information regarding the distribution and purchase of
digital editions is available from Digital Manager CK Russell
at digital@gomanga.com.

Seven Seas and the Seven Seas logo are trademarks of
Seven Seas Entertainment. All rights reserved.

Follow Seven Seas Entertainment online at
sevenseasentertainment.com.

TRANSLATION: Michael Rachmat
ADAPTATION: C.A. Hawksmoor
COVER DESIGN: Kris Aubin
INTERIOR LAYOUT & DESIGN: Clay Gardner
COPY EDITOR: Stephanie Cohen
PROOFREADER: Meg van Huygen
LIGHT NOVEL EDITOR: T. Burke
PREPRESS TECHNICIAN: Melanie Ujimori, Jules Valera
PRODUCTION MANAGER: Lissa Pattillo
EDITOR-IN-CHIEF: Julie Davis
ASSOCIATE PUBLISHER: Adam Arnold
PUBLISHER: Jason DeAngelis

ISBN: 978-1-63858-649-4
Printed in Canada
First Printing: May 2023
10 9 8 7 6 5 4 3 2 1

CONTENTS

CHAPTER 1
Fran and the Thieves' Guild   9

CHAPTER 2
Rescuing Garrus   67

CHAPTER 3
Blood on the Streets   121

CHAPTER 4
Clash of the Titans   183

CHAPTER 5
Black Cat Saint   231

CHAPTER 6
King Granzell   273

Epilogue   331

EXTRA CHAPTER
Fran the Ripper   341

1

Fran and the Thieves' Guild

SIDE: FREDERICK

"Here?"

"Arf."

"This room is empty... You're sure the young lady was here?"

"Woof!"

Jet, Fran's familiar, nodded to answer my question. He was an advanced familiar and had no problem understanding my words. We parted from the main group outside of Marquis Aschtner's mansion and went to save Velmeria.

Jet's nose was incredibly sharp, and he immediately led us to a mansion in the noble district. It belonged to a minor noble—a gift for allying themselves with Aschtner. There was no barrier, which made it all the more suspicious.

We entered the mansion and sensed no signs of life. There weren't even any servants around. However, the mansion looked lived-in, so it was definitely in use. Jet and I headed inside. Between his nose and my Scouting Skills, we quickly found the mansion's hidden paths.

Those paths carried us to a secret chamber where the sun didn't shine. It was outfitted with suspicious concoctions and contraptions, which looked out-of-place in a noble house like this. Large magic circles were drawn on the ceilings and floors, and the Mad Faith Sword was neatly tucked away in a corner. Marquis Aschtner was conducting strange experiments here, to be sure.

Velmeria was nowhere to be found, but her scent was fresh enough for Jet to pick up on it. We had just missed her.

"Can you find any sign of her?" I asked.

Jet sniffed the air. "Arf!"

"A piece of metal? It *is* emitting peculiar mana..."

Jet pointed his nose at a shard of metal on a shelf. It appeared to be a broken piece of a sword, but it was still emitting a powerful mana.

"Hang on to this, Jet."

"Woof."

Apparently, Jet could hide things away in his shadows. I didn't know whether that broken sword could take us to Velmeria, but it might be evidence of the marquis' crimes.

"Anything else?"

"Grrr!"

"What...?!"

Just as we were about to canvas the room further, Jet leapt up and pinned me down. For a moment, I thought he had betrayed me, but his hostility was pointed at someone else. Blood dripped from the wolf's body.

"What on earth...?!"

"Hee hee hee! Nice job taking the hit, pup!"

Jet growled again, and a chorus of shrill laughter echoed through the room. We were surrounded! And I didn't even notice our enemies waiting for us! I quickly got up to get a visual on our enemy, but when I did, it left me speechless.

Or rather, *she* did.

"Velmeria...?"

"What? You know who we are?"

"Huh...? Who are you?!"

Standing before us was exactly the person we were looking for. But, even if she looked like Velmeria, she felt nothing like her. Even just standing there, she exuded a sort of violence—her face twisted into a cruel expression. Even her voice was distorted.

Was this really Velmeria? Or was it a shapeshifter wearing her visage? My intuition said "no." Like it or not, the one standing before us really was Velmeria. In body, at least.

"Me?" she asked. "Let's see. Who am I?"

"What?"

"Tell me, who am I?"

"Velmeria, what are you talking about?"

"Grrrr!"

"Ha ha ha! Man, I wish I knew!"

Whatever was inside Velmeria let out a wicked laugh, and the room filled with repulsive mana. The hairs on the back of my neck stood on end.

That was when I knew the strength of our enemy.

That was when I knew that we couldn't win.

I knew what I had to do.

"Jet, get out of here! I'll keep it occupied!"

I was entrusted with Jet's care. I couldn't let him die here!

"Woof...!"

Fortunately, Jet complied and sunk into the shadows. He wasn't about to attempt any heroics—fighting an enemy he couldn't defeat.

The creature chuckled. "Not so fast!"

"Tch!"

I took the brunt of the next hit as the creature attacked the shadows.

"Do you mind?" she said. "I was in the middle of something!"

"You're not leaving this place."

"So that's how it's going to be. Anyway, what was that just now?" she asked. "It looked like you completely deleted my attack..."

"A fine question."

"Hee hee! So, you've got a trick up your sleeve! I can sense Malice from you. Is that the answer?"

My Drakefiend Halfling abilities allowed me to erase other people's magic. Technically, I could bend the rules of mana rather than the mana itself. Advanced Fiends sometimes possessed the same power. It was difficult to figure out at first, but my enemy knew what it was immediately.

Nullifying her attack had taken a lot out of me. I probably had two or three charges of it left. I needed to keep the creature talking and buy Jet more time. I could always teleport out of here if need be—provided this thing didn't kill me in one hit.

Suddenly, the creature's expression shifted.

"Hey...did you take the piece of metal from the shelf?" she asked.

"I'm not sure I follow."

"Don't play dumb with me, you bastard! Holy Order's fragment! Where is it?!"

"You're talking nonsense!"

"Well, I guess I'll have to beat you up then! Hope you don't die!"

"I won't die so easily!"

* * *

We left the Aschtner mansion and started making our way back to the guild. Along the way, we came across a scene of terrible carnage. A swordsman was burning the area down with Flame spells. He had a Fanatix replica plunged into his back, and these weren't your ordinary Flame spells, either. A single cast took no time at all and produced multiple explosions. Even a single one was enough to destroy several buildings, so the wooden houses in this district didn't stand a chance. Frightened screams filled the streets as people tried to get to safety.

"Bastard!" Erianthe shouted as she leapt into action.

The grim look on her face told me that she was prepared to sacrifice herself to buy more time for her people. The guildmaster knew she couldn't defeat the fanatic. It was uncertain if she'd even last long enough to buy them any time.

It's in Godsword Release...! What is going on?!

The sword driven the fanatic's back had been unleashed for some reason. It was so strong that, before I Identified it, I thought it was the real Fanatix. Replica or not, that sword still possessed Godsword Release—the fanatic's overwhelming power was proof enough of that.

"Stop that!"

"Raaaagh!"

A shock wave burst out of the swordsman and blasted Erianthe over ten meters away, into a wall. She managed to shield herself with her greatsword, but the impact was strong enough to split her blade in two. And still the fanatic wasn't done with her. He followed his attack up with a barrage of No-Cast Flame spells. A single fireball was enough to burn a human to ashes, and Erianthe had nowhere to run.

Dammit!

I flew into the fray, using telekinesis to scatter the Flame spell. I wish I could've protected her from further away, but I was still spent from the Aschtner fight. To deal with the spells properly, I needed to be up close.

"Huh? What just happened?" Erianthe said, watching Fran's sword float around on its own.

Well, time to go all in!

I created a doppelganger and directed it to appear in

front of Erianthe. It looked suspicious as all hell, but I wasn't about to reveal my true identity!

I cast a Wind spell around the clone for dramatic effect and had it grab me by the hilt. For Erianthe and the others, it looked like a mysterious man had appeared out of nowhere.

Be not afraid. I'm a friend of Fran's.

"You're the master of curry!"

Colbert had only met me once, but he remembered. As soon as Erianthe heard him, her suspicions disappeared.

Fight him head-on and you'll die. You know this, don't you?

"Yes, but even so...!" Erianthe protested.

I'll handle it. I may not look like much, but I taught Fran everything she knows. You look after her in the meantime, all right? I'm counting on you!

"Hey, wait—"

The fanatic was staring at me now, so the time for arguments was over. I left Erianthe and Colbert behind and jumped into battle. I hoped that they wouldn't waste time arguing with each other, and the adventurers didn't disappoint. They recognized the situation they were in and retreated from the battle immediately.

Now I just need to keep him occupied until he self-destructs.

Red beams rained down on me. Focused Flare Blasts, and twenty of them, and all at the same time. This fanatic's mana control was absurd! Even if Fran and I worked together, we couldn't cast this many.

The beams melted the stone buildings and they exploded, leaving holes everywhere. Fortunately, I was left unscathed. I had recovered just enough mana to use Dimension Shift.

Wind whirled around me, quickly turning into a tornado as the fanatic turned a Wind spell against me. The storm picked up rubble, gaining speed and growing in size. If I let the tornado develop further, it would ruin the whole city. I teleported and Air Hiked my way up into the sky, exposing myself to danger. The fanatic probably thought I was completely defenseless, but his expressionless face showed no sign of surprise. Still, I managed to get his attention, and that was enough.

The Inferno Bursts fused and amplified each other, creating a giant pillar of flame all around me. It was the same attack the P.A. had used back in the Lich fight, except this was several times more powerful. But, even in the midst of such terrible firepower, Dimension Shift ensured that I made it out unharmed. That spell took up a lot of mana, but I only had to sustain it for a few moments.

Meanwhile, the stress of Godsword Release was rapidly draining the fanatic's health and mana. He only had a few more minutes left at best. More time for civilians to get to safety.

Tsch!

I fired a weak Thunder spell at the enemy. It wasn't strong enough to damage him, but it was enough to keep his attention on me. As expected, the fanatic struck back by summoning a volley of exploding fireballs around me.

KABOOM!

Flare Explode activated, and the sky was filled with fire. It probably would have looked quite pretty to a bystander, assuming you were watching from a distance, that is. All the while, Dimension Shift kept me safe. It really was a useful spell, even considering its cost.

Missed me!

I provoked the fanatic with another attack, and he retaliated with another explosion, but it was pointless. His decision-making capabilities were lost in his berserk state. If he were smarter, he would realize that his attacks weren't working. The fanatic was more powerful than an A-Rank adventurer, but he was dumber than a reckless greenhorn. Keeping him occupied for a little while longer wasn't going to be an issue.

That's right, buddy. Just keep shooting fireworks into the sky!

Still, my Timespace Magic was the only thing keeping me alive right now. The other people in the city might not be so lucky...

Three minutes later, the fanatic ran out of life just as I was starting to worry about my mana reserves. He stopped moving, and his eyes stared blankly into the sky. He wasn't going to be a threat any longer. That had been the longest three minutes of my second life. I sighed and turned off Dimension Shift. The fanatic's attacks were so brutal that I activated the spell before they hit. If he had lasted just ten seconds longer, I would've had to start teleporting randomly instead.

Just as I was beginning to relax, it happened.

BOOOOOOM!

Whoa!

A sudden explosion. The blast was so powerful that the wind shook me, even as I floated in the air.

Dammit, the clone disappeared!

The explosion flung the rubble of ruined houses all around me. I panicked, doing my best to evade them while storing away the larger pieces. I thought the fanatic had come back to life and started blasting Flame spells again, but this time, the explosion was caused by an excess of mana. Apparently, the mana stored up in the Fanatix replica had nowhere to go after the soldier died, so it gushed out in all directions.

From the sky, I saw a gigantic crater where the fanatic used to be. The explosion destroyed everything around him—flattening the fifty houses at its epicenter and devastating the whole district. Hundreds of houses were damaged by the shock wave alone, and that wasn't all it did.

As I floated back to the ground, explosions sounded around the capital and pillars of mana rushed up into the sky. I guess my fanatic soldier wasn't the only one to burn out in an explosive manner. I counted over fifty explosions. Most of them came from the noble district, but the common and business districts weren't spared, either. The greatest of the explosions were clustered near the palace, and a lot of mana was whirling around that place.

What do they want? They're not suicide bombers!

Was the destruction of the capital their main goal?

Please be okay, Fran...!

As the explosions continued, I searched for her presence. Our mana was linked, so we could still sense each other's auras, even if we were miles apart.

Fran was still alive, but I couldn't tell if she was safe. Using the information from my search, I teleported myself to her.

The Adventurer's Guild.

Fran and the others had made it there.

"Wh-what?!"

Stellia, the guild receptionist, was startled at my sudden arrival. She was decked out in the red armor of her glory days and wielding a giant mace. She might be a bit wider now than the last time she wore it, but her armor had size adjustability. Once you got some quality enchanted equipment, you really were set for life.

Meanwhile, I was panicking a little. I should've teleported higher up in the air so I could sneak into the building unnoticed. Still, I wasn't about to explain the truth to Stellia. Instead, I flew inside the lobby and found Fran sleeping on the sofa. I moved quietly to her side, setting down beside her pillow.

Good to see you're okay.

Fran was sleeping soundly, her breathing regular. She was exhausted from the intense battle, but she'd be back to normal after she got some rest.

Stellia stared at me with her mouth agape. Was she suspicious? She might not think I was an Intelligent Weapon, but she might wonder if I was cursed, or a mimic in the shape of a sword. Who knows, maybe mimics were smart enough to camouflage themselves as a sword and track down their owner.

Please! I'm an innocent sword with a return function, I promise!

"Hmm," Stellia stared at me.

...

"I should check it to be sure."

I knew it! I just had to make sure that I didn't move!

My heart raced as Stellia picked me up to examine me, but someone else stayed her hand.

"That sword's all right, Stellia," Colbert said.

For some reason, he looked sad.

"You're sure?"

"Yeah. It's Fran's sword, after all. Her beloved master left it to her..."

His voice was shaking, and I was sure that he was getting misty-eyed.

"So," Colbert sniffed. "This is the Master of Curry's last will and testament."

Wait... My last will and testament?

Oh. My clone was missing, so Colbert assumed the sword had returned to Fran on its own. He thought the master of curry perished in battle against the fanatic.

Stellia sighed. "So, this is all that's left of him."

"Yeah."

No! I'm not dead yet, dammit!

Of course, I couldn't explain myself, so I settled for complaining.

"You will be missed, Master of Curry..."

"Curry?"

In the midst of this tearful mood, the word "curry" pulled Fran from her slumber.

"Curry..."

She scanned the room, looking for her favorite food. Instead, she found me next to her pillow.

"You're back," she said, with a look of relief only I could decipher.

She reached out to me and held me tight to her chest.

Everything go okay?

Hm... I noticed you were missing halfway through.

Fran woke up while Erianthe and Colbert were moving her. Even when she was asleep, she knew that I was no longer by her side. She knew that I was all right thanks to Skill Sharing, but the fact that I was gone still worried her. She closed her eyes and sighed, caressing my blade.

"I'm sorry for your loss, Fran," Stellia said, her voice wavering.

Colbert blew his nose. "Your master was a true hero...!"

The two of them rubbed their eyes. They couldn't tell what Fran was feeling, but they were trying to be strong for her.

Uhh, Fran...

I was about to ask her to explain when someone entered the room.

"You're awake."

"Erianthe."

"I hate to be the bearer of bad news, but there have been further developments," Erianthe said.

The stern look on her face told me that, whatever she had to say, it was important. Explaining my circumstances to Colbert and the others could wait.

Erianthe explained that fanatic soldiers were blowing up all over the place. The city was in shambles. Meanwhile, the outskirts were being terrorized by Marquis Aschtner's soldiers and mercenaries. The ensuing pandemonium was unprecedented.

"What about Garrus and Velmeria?" Fran asked. "Are they safe?"

"I don't know."

"So, you don't know where they are, either?"

"This is all I've been able to learn. It's chaos out there."

"Oh."

Fran nodded and stood up from the sofa.

Fran, what are you doing?

"I'm going to look for Garrus and Velmeria."

"Slow down, Fran," Erianthe said. "It's dangerous outside."

"She's right," Colbert added. "You deserve some rest after that fight."

Fran shook her head. "I'm fine."

They're right, Fran. We're too exhausted. We're in no condition to fight.

"I know it's dangerous out there," she said. "But someone has to find Garrus and the others."

If anything, the chaos outside only motivated Fran further. Between the walking fanatic time bombs and Aschtner's men, she had every right to be worried.

"And how do you plan to look for them?" Colbert said. "Are you just going to search at random?"

"Hm," Fran nodded. "We don't have any leads, so it's my only option."

She was seriously going to canvas the whole capital. Still, as much as I wanted her to rest, I doubted she would take my advice.

Erianthe sighed and shook her head at Fran's resolve. "I guess I can't stop you, but the capital is bigger than you think, and you don't know this place well enough. The odds of you finding them are nil."

"I'm still going to look," Fran said.

"I know, and I have no plans of standing in your way. Still, it wouldn't hurt to ask around for leads."

"You have someone in mind?" Fran asked.

"I do. Stellia, could you contact Face, please?"

"But guildmaster!"

Stellia protested, and given the look on Erianthe's face, she wasn't too enthusiastic about it either. Who was this Face person?

The receptionist shook her head. "I suppose you're right. Now's not the time to sweat the details."

"Thank you."

"I'll go and get him."

Five minutes later, Stellia returned with the man in question. He was short and not much of a fighter, but apparently he possessed the information we needed.

"Well, if it isn't Lady Erianthe," the man said sarcastically. "To what do I owe the pleasure?"

Erianthe's frown deepened. Whoever this man was, she didn't like him. Still, she held back her annoyance and introduced him.

"Fran, Colbert, this is Face. Adventurer and member of the Thieves' Guild."

"What?"

Colbert stared at Face, surprised. Face didn't seem too pleased about Erianthe telling us his identity, either.

"Lady Erianthe," he said. "It troubles me that you are so casual with people's private information."

"Shut up," Erianthe said. "We're in a hurry."

He sighed. "Very well."

Erianthe glared at Face with murderous intent. I almost felt sorry for him. The guildmaster was still in a bad mood, although she was better now that she'd blown off some steam. Erianthe explained that Face was the intermediary between the Adventurer's Guild and the Thieves' Guild. That position didn't win him any favors with the guildmaster.

There was an unspoken rule that the two guilds would stay out of each other's ways, but they were bound to brush up against each other from time to time. There were intermediaries like Face in both guilds. Some of them even had permanent memberships, but only the higher ups knew about them.

Identifying him revealed a wealth of Scouting Skills. His real name wasn't Face, either—that was just a codename.

"I have an urgent request," said Erianthe. "Assemble the council and tell them to hand over the information I want. I know they have it."

Face was silent for a moment. "Right away."

Despite Erianthe's thinly veiled threat, he nodded

with the same unfazed look. He knew that trying to save face right now would do more harm than good.

"Will you be the one meeting with them?" Face asked.

"They'll be seeing that girl over there," Erianthe pointed. "Fran the Black Lightning Princess. You've heard of her."

"So she's the one... All right. I'm sure the council wouldn't refuse."

What was *that* supposed to mean? Did the Thieves' Guild already know about Fran? Maybe they found out about her after she ran into Calc.

"I will arrange the meeting immediately," Face said.

He bowed and quickly left the room, but Colbert didn't look too happy about the arrangement.

"Are you sure we can trust the Thieves' Guild, guildmaster?"

"No," Erianthe said. "But I'm sure they will help. They don't want to lose the capital, either."

She sounded pretty confident about it.

"And you're sending Fran to meet them?" Colbert asked.

"Well, I can't leave the guild alone, can I?"

"Still," Colbert protested, "I could've gone with her."

"You have somewhere you need to be," Erianthe said. "If things go well, we can add more to our ranks."

"What?"

"Ever heard of the mercenary company Feeler and Shell?"

"Can't say I have. Actually, I've never heard of mercs working in the capital."

Mercenaries normally operated in the borderlands, going from battlefield to battlefield. That made it easier for the warring nations to hire them. Inland, there were fewer wars, and so mercenary companies were harder to find. At best, they left their liaisons and logistics personnel there on standby.

"They're an elite squad," said Erianthe. "Founded by an insectoid halfling."

"Old friends of yours?" Colbert asked.

Erianthe had told us about her history on the way back from the Aschtner mansion. She mentioned how she was a survivor of a doomed mercenary band and said that, after that fateful mission, her other comrades carried on with their work.

"That's right," Erianthe nodded. "I'll give you my recommendation. That will let you see their leaders. After that, it's all on your negotiating skills. They have a strict rule about not bringing children into battle, so it's better to send you rather than Fran."

Colbert sighed with relief. "That's good news! So, I'm

meeting the mercenaries while Fran goes to the Thieves' Guild, and ideally, we'll come out of it with more intel and firepower?"

"Exactly."

Erianthe had her hands full gathering adventurers, but I wasn't sure that sending Fran to the Thieves' Guild was the best idea. Would that really work out? Maybe I should make another clone, just to be safe.

We're dealing with the Thieves' Guild, Fran. Don't let your guard down.

Of course.

The guild probably couldn't offer us fighters, but they might have information that could help. In fact, they might have eyes and ears on both the marquis and the count, even amidst all the chaos. And, of course, they might know where Garrus and Velmeria were.

Face returned to the Adventurer's Guild not ten minutes later. Considering how quickly he got everything arranged, he must be pretty competent. Either that, or the Thieves' Guild just acted fast.

"Sorry to keep you waiting," said Face. "If you'll follow me?"

"Hm."

"We'll be taking some detours to avoid the riots. Stay close."

Face turned down one of the many alleyways of the capital. It was completely deserted. His chosen route had already been evacuated by the Thieves' Guild, so it was also free of Aschtner's cronies. That was information collection and manipulation at its finest, and the Thieves' Guild was excellent at it.

Face led Fran to a familiar-looking building—the pub where I issued a quest to Calc. This time, we entered through the back door.

"Can we come in?" Face asked the guard.

"Go ahead."

The guard cast a glance at Fran but didn't say anything. She was Face's guest, after all. We entered the building, and Face led us into a small, private room.

A small, private, *empty* room.

"Here?" Fran asked.

"One moment, please."

He closed the door and pulled a bit of string dangling next to it. Immediately, the wall on the other side opened, revealing a stairway down.

"Whoa!"

Fran beamed. There was something about hidden paths that screamed adventure.

Face walked us down the stairs into a sizable meeting room. A gorgeous round table was in the center. It could seat around ten people, but there were only three waiting for us. I had no idea if we'd come out of this meeting as friends, so I quickly Identified them. They weren't really the fighting types, but they all had interesting skills.

In the middle was a scarred bald man who looked like a traditional bandit. His skillset was a lot like that of an adventurer scout, but he had Charisma and Command Skills to support his position as a leader. He also winced as soon as Fran entered the room. As the muscle of the group, he knew how strong she was.

The good-looking man to his left was in his early thirties and a total marriage swindler. He had Acting Skills, as well those that helped him lie and intimidate. He could use magic, and even had Sexual Enchantment and the title Ladykiller. The bastard reminded me of Seldio.

To his right was an alluring woman who could pass for a madam. She had plenty of skills to seduce men, as well as those related to poisons. A poisonous prostitute? Well, that was absolutely terrifying!

Face bowed. "I shall take my leave."

"Good work," said the man in the middle. He waited until Face's aura disappeared before continuing. "Th-the name's Fist."

He wasn't so confident now that he had to deal with

Fran. Fist's companions thought that he was acting strangely, but they still put on their best smiles.

"I'm Honest."

"And I'm Pink."

They were very friendly, considering they were the Thieves' Guild's top brass, but their friendliness was fake. They were all using aliases too. Understandable, I guess, since they were all criminals. Fist the bandit, Honest the marriage swindler, and Pink the prostitute. Fitting names, really.

"Fran. Adventurer."

Fist nodded. "N-nice to meet you."

Sweat poured down his face and his eyes darted around the room. While this place seemed otherwise empty, I could detect multiple auras around it. The guild had *definitely* posted guards behind hidden doors. Fist wondered whether those guards would be enough to contain Fran if things went south and decided that they wouldn't be. Ironically, his composure returned as he resigned himself to that.

"We were thinking of reaching out to you too," he said. "W-we would've done it, even if the situation wasn't so dire. Anyway, please have a seat."

Did the Thieves' Guild have their eyes on Fran from the start?

"What do you mean?" she asked.

"We'll get there, but let's talk for a little bit. Break the ice."

"I don't have time to waste."

"We won't waste your time, then. Isn't that right, Honest?"

"Oh, you want my help now?"

Honest raised his eyebrows. He didn't seem to be expecting it and clearly didn't trust his fellow guildsman.

"This is too much for me," said Fist.

"She's that strong?"

"Listen," Fist said. "Don't piss her off. Not if you wanna live. My Danger Sense is pinging harder than the last time I met Hundred Blade."

So, that was the plan. Honest usually played good cop after Fist's bad cop act. However, Fran's power meant that Fist had zero chance of pressuring her, so he tagged Honest, who started talking with a brilliant fake smile.

"All right. How about you make yourself comfortable and have a drink, young lady? You must be parched from your trip."

"Don't need one," said Fran. "There's no time."

"Come on," Honest said. "A good negotiation can't start without a drink."

"I said I don't have time to waste."

"I just wanted to know you better." Honest laughed nervously. "It isn't every day I get to meet someone this beautiful and powerful."

He flipped his hair and gave Fran a megawatt smile. Back in Japan, he could easily have become the number one man in a host club, but Fran remained unamused.

"Don't you wanna chat a while with me?" he asked.

This was probably Honest's trump card when dealing with women. A smile from a man this handsome could make any girl swoon. No wonder he was the Thieves' Guild's top negotiator.

Fortunately, Fran wasn't interested in good looks! If anything, Honest's pointless detours only irritated her—especially given the urgency of the situation.

Still, Honest couldn't read her, so he kept smiling away. There was a hint of panic in him now, but he was able to maintain his smile all the same.

"W-wait!"

Tink.

An uncomfortable shock went through my brain. It was a familiar feeling. Back in Ulmutt, a thief called Solus used a skill called Coercive Influence, which produced similar effects. Honest was probably using Sexual Enchantment—a skill that enticed members of the opposite sex to listen.

Fran squinted. While she didn't recognize the skill back in Ulmutt, she was much more sensitive to it now. She kicked the floor and leapt over the table, landing smack in front of Honest. I didn't know whether she did it to intimidate him, but the table was visibly dented.

Fran drew her blade and pressed it against his neck, glaring at him with cold eyes. Honest was speechless, so the other two did the talking for him.

"Wh-what's gotten into you?!"

"Y-yeah! You can't just do that in a negotiation!"

"But using a skill is perfectly fine?" Fran asked.

Honest's gasp caught in his throat. He wasn't expecting Fran to see through his ruse. Any normal person would've apologized at that point, but people like Honest had a strange sort of pride. They couldn't accept losing at the negotiating table, and so this sort of behavior was a grave offense to them.

"H-how dare you draw your blade here! You'll regret that!"

"Will I?" Fran asked.

"Don't think you'll get out of the capital unscathed after making an enemy out of us!"

Aaaand now he'd done it.

Despite Fist's warnings to not anger Fran, Honest couldn't help judging her by how she looked. Or maybe he was just angry because his good looks and charm had failed. He tried to regain the upper hand by threatening her, but Fran only glared back at him. Honest was one wrong word away from getting his head cut off.

I could feel the tension rising behind the walls too. Even if the guards couldn't tell how strong Fran was, they trusted Fist. That was enough to prove she could wipe them out in an instant. But if Fist gave the order, *they* were the ones who would have to deal with her. Ah, the tragic life of a crony. I was sure that they were silently cursing Honest for being so stupid.

Either way, this wasn't how they wanted things to go. If it went on like this, things were liable to end before they could begin. Maybe I should've sent in a clone, after all. I certainly didn't want to get on the Thieves' Guild's bad side.

Still, before I could stop Fran, someone else stepped in.
"Wait!"
"Blergh!"

Fist rammed his fist into Honest's face to shut him up. Honest was sent flying in a tailspin and slammed into the wall. His chest was heaving, so he was still alive, but his face was in a terrible state. Considering it was his main moneymaker, he should probably get healed before those scars became permanent.

Fist got on his hands and knees to apologize. If his face had hit the floor, it would've been just like a Japanese dogeza.

"P-please! We're sorry! That was entirely his fault! He's always like that! We have no intention of making an enemy out of you, so please calm down!"

Fist and Honest were the same rank, so could he really talk about him like that? Pink had also lost her composure, and there was a tinge of panic in her voice.

"Wh-why did you do that, Fist?! Honest's guys might come after you for this."

"I don't care! It's better than getting slaughtered here! This girl's the real deal. The rumors were true!"

Fist would rather feud with Honest than face down an angry Fran. I don't know what kind of rumors he heard about Fran, but he was terrified of getting slaughtered by her. He held his head in his hands and started mumbling.

"This is why I didn't want a madam with no skills to be on the council! How is she supposed to help in this situation?! We're screwed!"

Pink sighed. "Has she really freaked you out *that* much? Fine. The men have proven to be utterly useless, so I guess you'll have to deal with me. I do hope you'll bear with me."

She smiled, despite knowing the danger Fran posed.

Still, Fran was feeling better after seeing Honest get punched into the wall. She nodded.

"Fine."

"Thank you."

Pink took a seat and Fran stepped down from the table, though she still had me in her hand. It wouldn't take much for Fran to finish Pink off, but despite knowing that Fran had all the cards, Pink didn't seem afraid. She definitely had the most guts on the council. She was more dragon lady than human woman.

"Since you're not one for small talk, I'll be frank. Garrus is no longer in Count Olmes' manor."

"What?!"

Fran hadn't even mentioned Garrus. Pink smiled upon seeing her surprise. It was good enough revenge for her.

"So," she said. "Now you're interested."

"How did you know?" Fran asked.

"Because information is our primary weapon. Also, we have a relationship with Garrus."

Pink shrugged and explained the situation. Apparently, the Thieves' Guild owed Garrus a favor.

"Once upon a time, one of our members got careless with a summoning manatek. It malfunctioned and ended up summoning a D-Threat monster in the middle of the city."

Garrus happened to be there and destroyed the manatek before it could summon more monsters.

"The authorities usually turn a blind eye toward us, but if they found out that we were summoning monsters here, the guild would've been shut down."

Suffice to say, the Thieves' Guild owed Garrus a big one. And, when they learned that Garrus was in Marquis Aschtner's custody, they made contact with him.

"The guild has people in the marquis' house?"

The Thieves' Guild really were worth their cut. Even while Bayreed's elites got caught, they remained unnoticed.

"We have our sources there," Pink said. "They mostly work for Aschtner, but they sell us little bits of information on the side. Even if we lost them, we lose nothing."

"I see."

"Although they do make it easy to sneak in. They won't open the door for us, but they can make sure that security is relaxed. That's all we need."

When the Thieves' Guild came to see Garrus at Olmes' mansion, he asked them for a favor. He had forged several scabbards in his isolation, and he wanted to post them up for auction.

"We couldn't say no. After all, we owed him. And besides, we got some nice weapons to auction into the bargain."

Apparently, Scabbard of the Teacher was listed in several auctions. Garrus couldn't know which of them Fran would attend, but he knew that she would visit one of them regardless. Besides, even if someone accidentally found his message, it was impossible to decipher.

So, why didn't the Thieves' Guild just send the message straight to Fran? Well, the guild had doubts about anyone new in town, and even if they didn't, the risk of an information leak was too great. Still, Fran was the only one who bid for their item, so their roundabout method worked out just fine. The guild must've kept eyes on all the scabbards that went up for auction.

All the same, I was amazed that Garrus managed to forge so many scabbards under lockdown. Apparently, the marquis gave him a workshop to keep his smithing skills sharp, so he just forged weapons and armor in his free time.

"Is Garrus all right?"

"Unfortunately, we don't think so. We had one of our members check in on him, and apparently they've been putting trace amounts of drugs into his food. Those drugs have recently taken effect."

Fran looked downcast. "I see."

"They also forced him to hold a broken sword from time to time," Pink continued. "He could still do his smithing work, but it seemed like he was doing it against his will by then. We think the drugs made him hallucinate."

The drugs must've been reducing his mental strength, allowing the Mad Faith Sword to manipulate him. From what we knew, the broken sword we encountered in the underpass was probably the true Fanatix. In Hummels' case, it had no qualms about destroying his psyche. All it needed was a host, but things were different with Garrus. Fanatix needed his intelligence, so they had to be careful of how much they drugged him. After all, craftsmanship was more than mere mechanical execution. It needed the craftsman's wisdom, sense, and personal genius, and all of those would be affected by a complete destruction of his mind.

"He was apparently moved to another location just the other day," Pink said.

"Where?" Fran asked.

"We think he's under a manor which used to belong to Baron Allsand, but we're not sure."

"Baron Allsand?"

The idiot noble who had Essence of Falsehood.

Fran looked like she vaguely remembered who he was. His father was Count Olmes, and Marquis Aschtner used Olmes's villa for his own purposes. It wouldn't surprise me if Aschtner used Allsand's former abode too.

"Go on," said Fran.

"Well," said Pink. "We know that Garrus was moved from the room he's been locked up in. The guild has eyes and ears in the Aschtner mansion, the Olmes mansion, and the Olmes villa, but they haven't seen him there."

"Hm."

"As such, it's highly likely that he was moved somewhere else."

"And you think it's Allsand's basement?" Fran asked.

"Yeah. Garrus is in an open space with lots of presumably human auras around him. That much we know for sure."

"Enemy guards?" Fran suggested.

"Most likely."

Wherever he was, he may well have been crafting more Fanatix replicas. We should expect heavy resistance when we get there. One fanatic soldier under Godsword Release was bad enough, but now we'd have to fight a whole squad? Then again, if these soldiers were unleashed, then they would have been blown up by now, so these guys were probably just ordinary fanatics. We should be able to take them.

"However," said Pink. "We don't know how to get to the underground chamber. We just can't find a way in, and not for lack of trying."

So, Garrus was either teleported in, or there was a cleverly hidden passageway somewhere. If it were the latter, it must be perfectly camouflaged—especially since it had escaped the notice of the Thieves' Guild.

"How do you know such a place even exists?" Fran asked.

Pink chuckled. "Rats can sneak into confined places just fine."

Wow! Was there no limit to the Thieves' Guild's spy network?

"How many do you have?"

"Sorry, but we don't exactly keep track of the rat population."

Oh.

So, the Thieves' Guild's 'rats' were just that: literal rats. Even the most confined of spaces had cracks in the wall, more than large enough for a rodent to squeeze through.

"But we have enough information to make an estimate of *their* numbers," Pink said. "There's less than a hundred of them."

"And how do you know that?"

"Well, you see—"

The Thieves' Guild had been keeping tabs on Marquis Aschtner and knew that the mercenary companies he'd hired over the years had been all wiped out.

"Not many things can wipe out merc companies," said Pink. "Especially not when we're not at war. Which begs the question: what happened to them then?"

The guild suspected that the missing mercenaries had been offered up as human sacrifices for some sinister ritual. And their suspicions were confirmed today, when they saw the marquis' guards being controlled by Fanatix replicas. Not only that, but the fanatic soldiers *also* attacked the guard posts where any implicated mercenaries were being held. Pink said there were eighty mercenaries involved with Aschtner. Add in the missing adventurers, and they would easily total a hundred.

"Do be careful," Pink said. "They'll be expecting you."

"Why are you telling me all this?" Fran asked.

The Thieves' Guild weren't exactly keepers of the peace, and I still didn't know why they were on our side. Honestly, I thought they would have sided with Aschtner. Then again, the marquis was dead now, so I guess the guild made the right choice.

"We don't want to lose the capital," Pink explained. "The Adventurer's Guild protects their hunting grounds and dungeons, and so we protect the city's seedy underbelly."

The Thieves' Guild had been here so long that they operated as intermediaries between the nobility and the commoners. As Pink said, the Adventurer's Guild had its dungeons and haunts, the Blacksmiths' Guild had its workshops and mines, and the Thieves' Guild had its capitals.

"We can't just move to another city if we lose," she said. "Everywhere else is already occupied. I guess top brass could go somewhere else, but what about your average guildsman? The pickpockets and burglars. The whores and gigolos. They'll have no choice but to be debt slaves."

I didn't know how many members of the Thieves' Guild there were in the capital, but there weren't enough jobs for all of them.

"Marquis Aschtner is no stranger to shady dealings," said Pink. "But he's completely lost it now. He's gone too far."

The Thieves' Guild were excellent information agents, all right. They knew something was wrong with Aschtner.

"We can't offer your additional firepower, but we can offer support in other ways. We're not even looking to get paid. We're all in this together, after all. What do you say?"

She's not lying, Fran. We can't completely trust them, but they're willing to cooperate.

"Hm. Good enough for me."

"So quickly? I knew I could count on you, Black Lightning Princess. We'll give you one of our guys as support. I promise he won't be a burden."

Teacher?

Just accept. They'll keep him on you, even if you refuse. We don't really have time to argue.

"All right."

Fran nodded, and Pink clapped her hands. It must have been some kind of signal, because a guildsman soon entered the room with an old man.

He was bald and had a shrunken frame. His eyebrows, mustache, and beard were long and white with age. If he weren't so seedy-looking, the old man could pass as a hermit. He was wearing a robe and carried a staff, which made me think he was a mage of some sort, but his hunched back suggested that he wouldn't be much use in a fight.

Still, looks aren't everything.

Before I could Identify him, Fran and I sensed the powerful mana radiating from within him. We readied ourselves, in case the old man tried to attack us. Being prepared would be the only way we could defend ourselves.

His mana wasn't the only menacing thing about him. He had the intimidating aura of someone truly powerful. Aschtner aside, he might be the strongest man in the capital. Even the late Skywall Zefield didn't come close. If the Thieves' Guild had someone like this on their roster, they really were a force to be reckoned with.

The old man noticed that Fran was on alert. "Oh, so you know how strong I am? You do your nickname justice. You're nothing like those idiots over there."

He muttered something under his breath, tapping the floor with his staff. He wasn't the friendliest senior citizen, that much was sure. His old eyes were sharp enough to silence a grown man.

"Meet the strongest man in the Thieves' Guild," said Pink.

"Name's Eiworth."

He was seventy-three years old. His Strength and Agility were low because of his age, but he was an elite mage with Storm Magic 3, Ocean Magic 2, Frost Magic 7, and Deadly Venom Magic 6. He could use Land Magic and Support Magic too, among other things.

Eiworth? I had heard that name before. Fran seemed to remember it too.

"You're one of Dias' friends?"

That was it! Eiworth was the name of one of Dias' old party members. The old man's eyebrow prickled with recognition.

"You know him?"

"Hm. I know Phelms and Gammod too."

"Is that right? Yes, I'm Dragon Bind Eiworth, and I was once a member of their party."

Despite the memories, Eiworth didn't smile. I wasn't sure if that was because they were no longer on good terms, or if it was just his personality. I mean, the guy had been frowning ever since he walked into the room.

"You made a weird secret organization too," Fran said.

"I made a what?" Eiworth wondered. "Oh, you mean the Mages' Guild."

"Hm. They were really annoying."

"I apologize for that. I did found that guild, but I'm no longer part of it. I lost interest, see? Their council are acting on their own now."

He's telling the truth.

Eiworth seemed to be the type who only did something as long as he was interested in it. As far as the old man was concerned, the Mages' Guild was nothing but a boring historical footnote.

I really wanted to tell him off for not settling things properly! Still, what was he doing in the Thieves' Guild? Fran was curious about this as well. She tilted her head, still keeping her guard up.

"What's a former A-Rank doing in the Thieves' Guild?"

"The old man used to be a bandit hunter," Pink answered for him.

Apparently, Eiworth showed up in the capital and

started attacking and abducting guild members. His reason? Human experimentation.

"I used to buy capital offense slaves, but that got expensive quickly. And they're not always available either," Eiworth explained. "That said, I can't just turn innocent bystanders into guinea pigs."

I thought that might be a sign he had *some* sort of moral compass, but Eiworth went on, explaining how messy things would've got if he got caught. And there I was, almost impressed with him for a moment!

"But then I had a revelation," said Eiworth. "Why not hunt thieves and experiment on them instead?"

That was the worst thing ever to hit the thieving industry, but the civilians benefited greatly. Still, he was hardly doing it for good reason. He just needed more guinea pigs.

"So," he said. "I started hunting garden-variety bandits."

After Eiworth began his hunting expeditions, the bandit population plummeted. Soon, the bandits all pulled their operations out of Granzell, deeming it too dangerous.

Then, instead of going to the mountains for more bandits or to the ocean for pirates, Eiworth decided to continue his hunt in the cities. It was inevitable that he'd run into the Thieves' Guild after that, but the guild didn't strike back at him. Instead, they negotiated a deal—giving him all the capital offense slaves and traitors he needed while hiring him as the guild's bodyguard.

"If the guild was under attack, then I could get all the subjects I wanted," he said. "Easiest job of my life."

Fran frowned. She didn't like Eiworth, and I didn't blame her. Then again, I didn't think that *anyone* could like him.

"I should add that I don't kill my test subjects," he said. "I just take a quick peek, heal them, and then release them. The capital slaves get resold, sure, but that's on them. Would you like to know about my findings?"

"No thanks."

Fran wasn't interested, and besides, we were in a hurry. Eiworth sighed, disappointed at her lack of curiosity. His eyebrows knitted together.

"Hmph. Everyone suddenly has a conscience when it comes to this stuff."

We couldn't let our guard down around him.

"He's a troublesome old man," said Pink, "but he's one hell of a fighter."

Fran looked pensive for a moment. "The enemy has a way of sealing magic and dispersing mana."

"What? Are you serious?"

"Hm."

Eiworth chuckled. "Very interesting."

"Hang on, Eiworth," Pink said. "As strong as you are, even *you* would have a hard time without magic."

Eiworth laughed all the harder. Clearly, Fran's warning had piqued his interest.

"I don't care. If I die, it's just because I'm weak, that's all. I've had my thoughts on that sword ever since the warnings came. It might help my research."

I was concerned about whether the old mage could help against such an enemy, but there was no stopping him now.

"Just try not to die out there," Fran said.

"I can handle it. Maybe."

He chortled, looking like a real villain. I don't think the Thieves' Guild trusted him either.

"Let's get going then," said Fran.

I didn't want Eiworth around, but he was definitely a force to be reckoned with on the battlefield. Even if we turned him down, he would just tail us anyway. Might as well have the old man where we could see him.

That's when Face came back into the room.

"Face will show you the way," said Pink. "You know the place, right?"

"That I do. It's chaos out there. Sneaking into the noble district shouldn't be a problem."

"How are things looking?" Pink asked. "Any sign of those freaks with the swords in their backs?"

"There's plenty of them. The knights are having a tough time."

That didn't surprise me. The fanatics were adventurers and mercenaries with Godsword Release. They were much stronger than any knight. Without skills or magic, the knights simply couldn't defeat them.

"The Adventurer's Guild has managed to gather twenty adventurers to support them, but I don't know how long they'll last. They're only intermediates..."

"Are they losing?"

"No. The guildmaster is requesting more adventurers and knights from the palace as reinforcements. They're doing better than before, at least."

I was curious about the situation near the palace, but we had Allsand's old mansion to deal with first.

"Are enemy reinforcements coming from whatshisface's basement?" Fran asked.

"No. There hasn't been any movement around the Allsand mansion."

Very suspicious.

Hm.

What was so important to that broken Godsword? Why hold back its forces like that? The only thing—or person—I could think of was Garrus. All the signs were pointing to him being captive in the mansion of the former Baron Allsand.

"Shall we?"

"Hm."

"A strange magic sword," Eiworth chuckled again. "I can't wait."

I was a little worried about the old man. If he kept underestimating our enemy, he would run into problems.

Still, Fran and the others left the Thieves' Guild, running through alleyways with Face in the lead. Despite Eiworth's age, he had no trouble keeping up. He used to be an A-Rank, after all. He didn't even break a sweat as he asked Fran about the Fanatix replicas. It was strange seeing a hunched old man running at such speed. He reminded me of a Japanese urban legend called the Turbo-Granny. She wasn't known to be dangerous, but just seeing her gave people the spooks.

The Allsand manor was in the southern part of the noble district. We were a good distance from the Aschtner and Olmes mansions, so there was no fighting here. I could hear the sounds of spells exploding and the desperate cries of knights in the distance, but we didn't run into a single adventurer or knight along the way. Face was deliberately avoiding them; he really was worth his weight here. He might not be strong in a fight, but he was not to be messed with. We reached our destination without as much as a glimpse of the conflict.

"Welcome to the Allsand mansion."

SIDE: BAYREEDS

What on earth is happening?
"Aaaaah!!!"
"Gaaaah!!!"
"Eeeergh!"

Velmeria, my beloved daughter, was demolishing my knights. Like Frederick, she had somehow developed blue scales all over her body, making her look more like her ancestors. But, despite her transformation, I still knew it was her.

With each swing of her arm, she fired giant balls of water at the knights. With each swing of her broken sword, she unleashed a shock wave that sliced through the adventurers.

"Come on! Keep pushing!"
"Dammit, I can't hit her!"
"How did she see that?!"

Despite my knights' best efforts, not one of them managed to land an attack. Velmeria dodged and blocked everything. Spells, arrows, spears... Everything. One of the attacks would graze her occasionally, but they bounced right off Valmeria's intense mana. My daughter was the enemy of the capital, and I had ordered my men to kill her. They had so far failed, but I was hardly happy about it. In fact, I was beginning to doubt whether this thing was my daughter at all.

"I'll rip all of you insignificant worms to pieces!"

She certainly looked like Velmeria, but it seemed like something else was inside her. Both her strength and her personality had changed.

"Hah ha ha ha! Die, die, die!!!"

The sounds coming out of her were neither male nor female. The noise was high-pitched and grated the ears. Something else was clearly in control of her body.

"General Bayreeds, what do we do?!" asked one of my platoon commanders, approaching me with eyes full of confusion.

The man's officer was supposed to report in to me, but that one had already fallen in battle. The platoon commander was actually asking two questions. First, what do we do about the increasing number of casualties? Second, would I give them permission to attack my daughter? Either way, my answer remained the same. It didn't matter if Velmeria was being controlled by something else.

"Keep on the offensive!" I shouted. "The palace is behind us! If she gets past, she might go after the king or slaughter civilians!"

The king and the civilians. The two things I'd sworn an oath to protect. As much as I loved my daughter, I had to do my duty.

"Y-yes sir!"

"There are bound to be mages amongst our reinforcements," I said. "Hang on until they get here!"

"Shouldn't we contact the palace for backup?" the field commander asked, looking at the palace behind us.

The royal guards were the cream of the crop. The strongest of the capital's knights. Their commander might be Granzell's strongest and most famous warrior—ranking amongst the likes of Hundred Blade and Hariti. But I couldn't ask for their help. Their place was by the king's side. Their mission? To protect him with their lives. Whether the capital was terrorized by a single enemy or an entire army, they had to stay with him. They were the king's shield. Eliminating threats and protecting civilians was *our* job.

"Can you see it, Starg?"

"Yes... Well, not completely but I cannot believe what I'm seeing."

Starg was one of House Bayreeds' knights, and my personal bodyguard. He was an elite fighter, and also possessed Identify. Still, it took time for him to completely analyze Velmeria. And, going by the pale shade of his face, things weren't looking so good.

"She's that powerful?" I asked.

"I hate to be rude, my lord, but your daughter is a monster."

Starg was no stranger to battle, but he was terrified. This was the same Starg who faced down a demidrake and fired an arrow between its eyes.

"First of all," he said. "I could not Identify the broken sword. Whatever it is, it's enchanted, and a powerful piece of equipment."

"I see..."

Is that the Sword of Mad Faith that the Black Lightning Princess mentioned? Fanatix? But it isn't lodged in her back...

"Secondly," Starg went on. "Although I could Identify Skywall Zefield, Lady Velmeria is too strong. I cannot grasp her full strength. Her total stats are over one thousand, at least."

"She's stronger than an A-Rank," I mused.

"She also has an absurd number of skills," said Starg. "Sword King Arts and Mastery, both at Level 8, Instant

Regeneration 8, and close to a hundred advanced Skills. She also possesses some Unique and Extra Skills. I can see Sword King Mastery, Shinryu Form, Flame Drain, Herculean, Skanda, No Cast, Mana Control, and Spirit Control, but she definitely has more."

Starg's list wasn't exhaustive. Velmeria possessed more rare and advanced skills. If I didn't trust him, I would've thought he was joking.

"That doesn't make sense," I said. "No one can get that strong in such a short time."

"She is currently in Fanatic and Shinryu Form. I think one of those is to blame for Lady Velmeria's current condition..."

Shinryu Form! I'd heard of it before. Tirananalia, Velmeria's mother, spoke of it when she explained draconian mythology. Shinryu were a powerful evolution of drakes, much like high elves were to elves. Although no one knew how to they evolved, there were historical records of several Shinryu over the last ten thousand years. Apparently, they once clashed with the high elves. According to legend, it ended in a draw.

This was a nightmare. As if it wasn't bad enough that Velmeria was an enemy of the state, now she was powerful enough to overwhelm A-Ranks. If the legends were true, then she should be as powerful as a high elf—on the same level as an S-Rank. But who knew what she was truly capable of as long as she had the Sword of Mad Faith? The Godswords worked miracles and defied reason. Mad Faith was powerful enough to turn an ordinary girl into a monster in an instant.

"Send word to the palace!" I cried.

"S-sir?"

"Tell them to evacuate the king immediately!"

"Yes sir!"

We had no chance of winning. Even if we brought several A-Ranks together, we could still lose. As far as I knew, the only ones currently in the country were Skywall Zefield, Hundred Blade Forlund, Black Lightning Princess Fran, Dragon Bind Eiworth, and Luga Moufle—Captain of the Royal Guard. To even stand a chance against Velmeria, I would have to gather them all together.

The palace wasn't safe, even with all its barriers. First, we had to get the king out of the way. After that, we'd just have to save all the civilians we could. Chances were, we would die in that endeavor, but it was the best that we could do—buying time for the others to get here.

"We'll hold her off for as long as we can," I said. "We might not make it out of here, but we have to fight. Lives are depending on it."

"Yes, sir!"

"Understood!"

The best thing about this situation was the resolve in the voices of my men. They would follow my orders unflinchingly, even if I ordered them to die. It was a shame that none of them would get out of here, but it couldn't be helped.

I sent some younger soldiers to carry my message to the palace. After all, they needed to know that defeating the enemy would require several A-Ranks together. After that, my fellow generals would know what to do, even if I died here as well.

"I'll fight too."

"Sir!"

"If only Master Dimitris was here," one officer mumbled.

"Sir Dimitris, eh?"

Dimitris the Indomitable. Jillbird's sole S-Rank adventurer. They said the martial artist had gotten his nickname after killing a hundred enemies in an instant and without even taking a single step. He operated out of his dojo in the south, but he often trained by visiting various haunts on the continent. He wasn't a friendly old man by any means, but he had a good heart, and he made a point to save people. Dimitris would certainly be willing to lend a hand here, but I didn't know whether he was even in the country.

"No use lamenting over people who aren't here," I said.

"I-I apologize, sir."

"That's all right. It's not like the thought hasn't crossed my mind. But we don't know where Sir Dimitris is right now, so it's up to us to protect the capital!"

"Sir!"

The officer reprimanded himself and was about to march to the frontlines when I heard a man's voice.

"I'm not Old Dimitris, but maybe I can help."

"Huh?"

A large ogrekin suddenly appeared behind me. How did he do that? I didn't so much as sense his presence! He was no ordinary man, to be sure. His aura reminded me of the Beast King.

The giant unsheathed the greatsword on his back, and it was no ordinary sword. Its mana was oppressive.

"Anyway, backup's arrived," he said. "Gravity Blow!"

The man swung his sword and the sky over Velmeria suddenly cleared. It was like an invisible force pushed down through the clouds. Velmeria's body slammed into the ground.

"Gaaaaah!"

It was the first time Velmeria had suffered significant damage. Who on earth *was* this man?!

"I wonder how long I can last..." the ogrekin muttered to himself.

Reincarnated as a sword

2

Rescuing Garrus

WE REACHED BARON ALLSAND'S former mansion and found it in a state of disrepair. Weeds sprouted all over the front lawn, while other parts had dried up after a month of neglect. Vines reached over the front gates, highlighting the dirtiness of the walls, and the flowers in the garden were sad and wilted. The situation was the same on the inside.

Count Olmes' son was undergoing treatment for his illness and had not returned to his mansion. At least, that was the official story. The *real* story was that he offended a member of the royal family after losing Essence of Falsehood, and the nobles and syndicates in the capital all knew it.

"The Thieves' Guild spread that rumor, in any case."

The Olmeses had played a lot of thieves in their time;

the guild had been waiting to spread malicious information about them.

"Apparently, Baron Allsand is in exile in a quiet corner of the country."

"Huh."

Fran didn't look interested in the least. We were to blame for what happened to the baron, but then again, he had it coming. Anyway, we had more important things to think about right now—like how to get inside that underground chamber.

Face stopped at a corner of the garden and tapped the ground with his foot.

"It's right below us."

"But we have no way of getting in," Eiworth said. "And no clues either, I take it?"

"No," Face said. "Our rat user couldn't find the path in either. Apparently, the rats got in through some tiny crack in the walls."

"I've never met this rat user. What do they do?"

"As I remember it—"

The rat user could sense the location of rats, peek through their memories, and read their surface-level thoughts. However, the rats lacked ample intelligence, so it was impossible to ask them detailed questions.

"Hmph," said Eiworth. "Sounds useless. I could blow

through the ground here with ease. A single spell should do it."

"I admire your enthusiasm," said Face. "But you really shouldn't. You might kill Garrus in the process."

"Fair point. This is quite the troublesome predicament."

We needed to find a solution before Eiworth did something ridiculous.

The room beneath us is big. I'm sensing signs of life too... and there's the disgusting aura of Fanatix replicas again.

My senses were attuned to it now.

Hm.

However, I couldn't tell how many there were. Certainly not a hundred. I'd guess somewhere between ten and twenty at least. Maybe I could get a better idea if we got closer.

Should we use a Land spell to tunnel through the ground? I could teleport us inside, but going in blind to fight an untold number of fanatics was too dangerous. Especially when Fran was exhausted. Only her sheer determination to save Garrus and Velmeria kept her on her feet. Under any other circumstances, she should still be resting. If at all possible, we should avoid intense fighting and rescue Garrus stealthily.

What if I teleported myself in first and culled the enemy ranks some?

As I pondered my options, Eiworth started casting a spell. The mana he was gathering was immense.

"Master Eiworth, what are you doing?!" Face shouted in surprise.

But Eiworth continued casting. By the time he was finished, there was a gigantic hole in the garden.

"They're going to notice us if we're not careful!"

"We can't exactly sneak into this place, can we?" said Eiworth. "Might as well get a look at this chamber."

"I thought this was going to be a stealth operation."

Eiworth shrugged nonchalantly. "It could still be, but we'll fight if we have to."

This guy was just doing whatever he pleased!

I peeked into the hole he'd made. It was pretty deep, with a faint glow shining at the bottom. It must've gone all the way down to the secret chamber. I had considered using Land Magic too, but nothing on this scale! The enemy would definitely spot us now!

"Looks like the spell reached our destination," said Eiworth. "There was an anti-magic barrier around it, but nothing I couldn't handle."

He seemed annoyingly calm as he threw something into the hole. Several somethings, in fact. They looked like bottles, but I couldn't be sure.

"What were those?" Fran asked, speaking for the first

time since Eiworth opened the hole.

"Some special chemicals. They turn into gas and spread immediately."

Chemicals? Like poison chemicals? But what if Garrus was down there?!

Fran glared at Eiworth. "Garrus could be down there!"

Eiworth chuckled. "Calm down. The chemicals won't kill anyone. One can paralyze people by causing severe pain on the skin, another corrodes metal, and the last one stimulates the mana core of living things to make them rapidly lose power."

"But..."

"The first potion causes paralysis and no more. It doesn't physical harm anyone. At most, it numbs your limbs for a short time. You can't die from mana exhaustion, and metal corrosion has no effect on humans. And besides, dwarves are naturally resistant to such concoctions. However, the guards with swords in their backs? They'll *definitely* be affected."

The first two concoctions didn't count as magic potions, even if magic was involved in their production. There was a high chance the fanatics couldn't nullify their effects. The mana sap potion *was* magic, but Eiworth had included it for a reason.

"To completely defend against these potions, they

will need to use Unleash Potential. That will exhaust our enemies before we have to fight them," Eiworth explained as we made our way to the chamber.

As egotistical as he was, the old man was first-class. Fran understood that, but she was still glaring at him. Eiworth didn't seem to care.

What's done is done. We should focus on our mission instead of being angry at him.

Hm...

Don't let your guard down. There's a chance we might have to go up against several squads of fanatics!

"Hm!"

Several minutes later, Fran and the others were inside the mansion, searching for a passage to the underground chamber. Technically we didn't need one, since we had Land spells and teleportation on our side, but Face said it was best to look for a proper way in regardless.

Fran and I used our Sensory and Exploration Skills to look for secret doors, but they turned up nothing. Maybe the entrance was somewhere outside the building? We turned back toward the gardens and sensed a powerful mana moving. It was a familiar signature now and, sure enough, by the time we came out of the building, Eiworth had dug up another hole.

"Eiworth!"

He looked genuinely puzzled at Fran's anger. "What is it, girl?"

"I told you not to do anything reckless," said Fran.

"Right, now that you mention it, you *did* say that before going inside. But I wasn't paying attention, so I forgot."

"Grrr...!"

Fran had warned him not to do anything rash, and Essence of Falsehood hadn't triggered, so he at least had been telling the truth then. Apparently, he had genuinely forgotten about the promise he made before they split up to investigate. I hadn't expected him to be this free-spirited...

"But never mind that," he said. "Let's get going. And don't worry about the potions—they should've expired by now."

Eiworth lifted his body with a Wind spell and headed straight down the hole.

"Hey!"

"Master Eiworth, no!"

But the old man couldn't resist the call of his own curiosity.

We're going after him, Teacher!

Right!

I thought about letting Eiworth handle the rest, but that could leave Garrus in genuine danger. Who knew if

Eiworth cared about anyone's safety—after all, he threw poison bombs down the hole. He hadn't even hesitated. If worse came to worst, he could even end up experimenting on Garrus.

"Eiworth, wait!"

"W-wait for me!" Face yelped.

Face struggled to keep up as Fran followed Eiworth down the hole. It was too deep for an ordinary adventurer to just hop down. Considering what we might be up against, perhaps it was best to leave Face behind.

Fran plummeted down the hole, killing her momentum with a last second Air Hop. The only thing left of Face were the echoes of his voice still coming from above. Fran set up a wind barrier in case Eiworth's potions were still in the air, but we were in the clear. The old man was right—his potions had expired.

"Man-made," Fran remarked.

Yeah, we're definitely in the secret chamber now.

It looked like we were inside a fortress. I didn't see Eiworth, so he must've gone on ahead.

Careful. You don't know where they're going to strike from.

"Hm."

We decided to follow Eiworth's trail for now, scanning the area as we ran down the passageway. I couldn't detect any signs of life, but I could feel the faint presence of the

Fanatix replicas. They must've been concealing themselves after Eiworth's dynamic entry. We finally caught up to him twenty meters down the passageway, where we found him standing in a large hall.

"What are you doing?" Fran asked.

"You made it. Have a look at this."

"Stairs?"

A spiral staircase led upwards from just ahead of us. I thought that it must connect this place to the outside world, but the stairs instead led straight up into the ceiling. Had they buried the staircase to hide this whole underground complex? No. When Eiworth charged the staircase with mana, it glowed.

"I knew it," he said. "Manatek."

Eiworth poured more mana into the staircase, and it glowed brighter where it touched the ceiling. Apparently, when it was fully charged, the staircase would open. That's why we couldn't find the entrance from above—someone needed to open the way from the inside. That would drastically reduce the risk of attack... But it wasn't like that mattered when faced against a battering ram like Eiworth.

"We'll investigate this later," he said. "Let's head over there."

"Hm..."

Fran nodded, although she wasn't completely on board. She didn't approve of Eiworth's reckless behavior, but she had to acknowledge the old man's knowledge of manatek. For now, she kept her complaints to herself and followed.

That's when I noticed the mana signatures ahead.

Fran! I'm detecting Fanatix replicas on the other side of that door. I think there's two of them!

Hm? Got it!

Fran stopped in front of the door. She hadn't noticed them herself, but then again, I was picking up on their disgusting aura rather than their mana.

"Eiworth."

"What is it? Did you sense something?"

"Hm."

Eiworth stopped and looked around. He still thought like an A-Rank.

"It's on the other side of that door," Fran said.

"Oh?"

Fran pointed to one of the doors in the hallway. Eiworth didn't sense anything, but he didn't let his guard down. He realized that her senses were sharper than his.

"The enemy?" he asked.

"I don't know, but there's two of them."

"I genuinely cannot tell," Eiworth mused. "You take point."

"Hm!"

He stepped back, and Fran kicked the door down. I already had a plan: the first guy would get hit with a Pressurized Quickdraw! Then we'd back off and launch a Telekinetic Catapult, using Eiworth as a shield if need be. The old mage should buy us enough time.

Fran charged into the room, sword drawn, prepared for anything. In so doing, she disturbed a black powder that had settled over everything. This was probably the armory. Eiworth's metal corroder must have rusted everything away, leaving nothing but black dust behind. The only things remaining were leather armor and shields, along with straps that had once been wrapped around sword hilts.

There were two men inside, both with Fanatix replicas in their backs, but I didn't get the chance to carry out Plan Eiworth Shield. By the time we stepped inside, they were already done for.

Fran approached the fallen men carefully. "Hm?"

They look dead...

Fran cut the swords out of their backs, but the soldiers remained motionless. Still, Cannibalize triggered, so they were *definitely* Fanatix replicas. Behind us, Eiworth entered the room.

"They're dead," he confirmed, disappointed.

Identify revealed that their life and mana were completely drained. Eiworth's potion must have been pretty effective. I didn't know whether those potions had done this on their own, or whether the Fanatix replicas had used all their mana trying to cancel out the effects. Either way, these guys were dry.

Perhaps they used Unleash Potential to try and combat the paralysis potion. Or maybe they couldn't use their mana nullifying abilities when Unleash Potential was activated. In any case, they were out of mana and so they couldn't regenerate their health. On top of that, the swords were weak—probably because they couldn't draw enough mana from their hosts.

"I was expecting them to be exhausted, but our enemies are bigger fools than I thought," said Eiworth, talking to himself as he inspected the bodies. "I suppose their decision-making skills went out the window when they were mind-controlled. Perhaps the swords show their powers under special circumstances? Aaah, but..."

The old man was lost in thought, but this was not the time for scientific inquiry.

Fran silently stored the bodies away.

"What are you doing?!" Eiworth said.

"We have to go."

He clicked his tongue. "Fine. But I'll have to look at those bodies later."

"......"

"Did you hear me, girl? I said I want to look at those bodies."

"......"

"What's gotten into you?"

Fran ignored him. She had decided that talking to Eiworth was a pain in the rear. He wasn't a good listener, and yet here he was, getting angry at Fran for ignoring him. The old mage was a class act.

"Did you hear me?" he asked. "I want to dissect those bodies."

"......"

"Why won't you say anything?!"

When Fran realized that he wasn't going to shut up about it, she gave him one of the bodies. I could almost feel her saying, "If you want it so much, fine." But Eiworth accepted it happily—he snatched the body out of the air as we ran and stowed it in his item pouch. He reminded me of a boy who had caught a rare bug. How revolting.

Eiworth chortled. "An excellent specimen. This could advance my research."

"......"

I had to give props to him for being able to annoy Fran like that.

We kept running until our surroundings finally started to brighten. There was another hall at the end of the passage, and I could sense more Fanatix replicas down there. The tragic scene we encountered in the armory was probably waiting for us there too.

The place is a pile of corpses.

"All dead?"

No. There are some still kicking.

I detected life signs from several of them.

"More of them, girl?" Eiworth asked.

"A few. Still alive."

"Is that so?"

Eiworth's eyes gleamed darkly. He was itching to get a close look at a live specimen.

Don't let your guard down.

Hm!

We entered a dimly lit hall. I was expecting a legion of fanatics, but there were roughly twenty of them, already dead. Only four were left standing. The survivors either had Poison Resistance or Wind Magic to defend themselves against the potions, but now they were almost out of mana and significantly weakened. This was our chance.

Go for it, Fran!

"Hm!"

Almost before I finished directing her, Fran launched me at our enemies. That's my Fran! Even when she was exhausted, she still made perfect decisions.

I accelerated using Telekinetic Catapult and smashed into the head of the woman in front, also targeting the Fanatix replica in her back.

Three left! I shouted.

Fran pulled me back to her hand using my strap. One tug was all it took.

Nice! Just as planned!

"Hm!"

Usually, I would just fly back to her, but my mana was disabled so I made sure to extend my strap beforehand. Things were going even better than expected.

Again, Teacher.

You got it!

"Haaaa!"

The hall was big, and our enemies' mana nullification hadn't reached the entrance yet. This gave us another chance at using Telekinetic Catapult. A fanatic soldier charged at Fran, and she responded by blowing his head off. It was almost a perfect repeat of what had just happened. Fran yanked my strap, and I returned to her side.

"Hey. Leave one for me," Eiworth butted in, just as we were about to eliminate the rest.

"Hrm."

I thought about ignoring him, but if we kept slighting him, then Eiworth might turn against us. No good could come out of that. Maybe we should let him do as he pleased for a bit. Besides, another fanatic was fast approaching, and we needed to make some space before we could use another Telekinetic Catapult.

Well, I guess we'll take this one and let the last one come after— I mean, let Eiworth handle the last one.

"Hm. Fine."

Fran nodded and attacked the neck of the charging dwarf fanatic. The strike was supposed to slice his head clean off, but the dwarf specialized in defense. Fran's sword struck a powerful barrier around his neck and bounced off. However, the dwarf wasn't very good at attacking, and Fran easily avoided his greatsword. Perhaps we should just let Unleash Potential run its course.

"I see the Black Lightning Princess doesn't need backup," Eiworth scoffed. "I'll take this one then."

He turned toward the last big man, more motivated now than ever.

"First, let's see how durable you are. Poison Fog."

"..."

"Ooh! Did you nullify my mana? I can't believe you dispersed a magically produced fog! Very interesting."

The old mage seemed pleased at how badly his fight was going. I was a bit worried for him. Mages couldn't do much once you took their mana out of the equation. Still, he carried on fighting the man joyfully, taking several bottles out from his robe and throwing them at his opponent. The large man exploded into flames.

"...!"

Fran jumped away and covered her ears in surprise. But even after that explosion, the big man was still standing and only slightly singed.

"I see," said Eiworth, laughing despite interrupting Fran's fight. "You cannot disrupt chemically induced phenomena because they aren't created by mana."

He cast another spell to freeze the surrounding area, but again, the fanatic soldier disrupted it.

"Uh-huh."

Eiworth nodded and weaved through the enemy's attacks, casting more spells. He threw multiple bottles this time, but the effect was the same. Their magical contents were nullified, and the only damage the enemy took was from breaking glass. Eiworth's efforts seemed to be for naught, but you wouldn't know it by the look on his face.

"Aaah, I see," he observed out loud, deeply interested. "So you can't specifically target the person whose mana you wish to nullify. Is there an area of effect then? You certainly didn't nullify my mana when I cast spells from a distance. The potions are little more than water now, and there are effects which remain unobserved. Which means…"

In just a few moments, Eiworth had managed to learn much more about the enemy's mana nullification powers. As much as I hated to admit it, his perception was top-notch. Still, Eiworth lacked a way to defeat his opponent. With both his mana *and* his potions rendered ineffective, he couldn't finish the fanatic off.

Even so, Eiworth avoided the big man's attacks easily, so the old man wasn't completely inept at melee range. He had several Combat and Evasion Skills, and while his stats might not be what they used to, his experience more than made up for it.

Eiworth continued to avoid the fanatic's attacks, taking out five more bottles. He broke them at his feet, releasing the gas within. I thought the smoke would cover them both, but it immediately dispersed. The potions were magical. The old man must be desperate if he was willing to use an attack that could harm him too, but Eiworth hadn't stopped smiling. If anything, he was overjoyed. Still avoiding his enemy's attacks, Eiworth started casting a spell, showing an immense focus. He raised his hand against his assailant with a smile on his face.

"Eternal Coffin."

"......"

What happened next was beyond our imaginations.

Huh?

"Hm? What happened?"

Fran and I were perplexed. Eiworth's spell took effect, and the man froze.

Wait, I get it.

Eiworth had used magic potions—forcing his enemy to use up the last of his mana nullification ability. Once it was exhausted, Eiworth simply hit him with a spell.

Fran, I think I've figured out an easy way to beat these guys.

Really?

Yeah. Hit them with Pressurized Quickdraw immediately after I use magic.

Got it.

I knew that the fanatics used their own magic to nullify mana, but I hadn't realized that I could use that to our advantage. That one was on me.

All right, let's go! Have fun nullifying these!

I fired off ten spells. As expected, all of them were nullified.

"Haaa!"

But immediately afterward, Fran launched a Pressurized Quickdraw at the dwarf's head, lopping it off and breaking the Fanatix replica in his back. It was all so simple. With my mana reserves, I could exhaust their mana nullification ability in a snap. That wouldn't work against a whole squad of fanatics, but it would help in individual encounters. Exhaust the enemy's mana, prevent them from buffing and healing themselves, and then finish them off.

Ugh, I can't believe I didn't think of this sooner. Oh well, I can mope about being dumb later. Let's look for Garrus.

"Hm."

"You don't mind me taking this one, do you?" Eiworth asked, pointing to the man encased in ice.

Fran remained silent, but he took her that as an endorsement. He stuffed the specimen into his item pouch.

Fran rolled her eyes. "Let's go."

Soon, we found a giant opening, where a huge door clearly used to be. It must've been made out of metal because we saw remnants of it scattered nearby. Eiworth's corrosive potion must have eaten through it. No matter how big or airtight it was, it didn't stand a chance.

We stepped through the door and found a prison on the other side—thick with the stink of death and melancholy. Using necromancy here would resurrect one hell of a grudge.

The prison was laid out in a neat grid, and there was no one around except for one guard, dead on the floor. Fran ran to one of the cells.

"Garrus!"

We finally found who we were looking for. I did a quick scan and found that he was merely unconscious.

"Huh?"

Fran pulled on the iron bars, but they didn't give. They seemed to be made of a special material since they'd resisted Eiworth's corrosive chemicals.

"Must be magic alloy," Eiworth said. "That potion doesn't work very well on them."

Fran took his advice and prepared an attack.

"Tsch!"

I cut right through the bars. Special alloy or no, they were no match for me now that there was nothing to hold my mana back.

Fran stepped inside and shook the unconscious dwarf. "Garrus, are you okay?"

"……"

There was no response. Even though Garrus was unconscious, he wasn't looking good. His skin was cold and his heartbeat was too slow. He seemed to be at death's door.

"Greater Heal! Garrus, can you hear me?"

No, he's not waking up.

It was probably the drugs they were feeding him and not Eiworth's potions. Probably.

Let's get him out of here.

"Hm."

Fran carried Garrus out of his cell. His dwarven body looked like it could crush the tiny catgirl, but Fran wasn't fazed. His weight didn't bother her, and I helped balance Garrus with Telekinesis.

Where's Eiworth?

"Hm?"

We found him squatting in front of the cell, examining the body of the fanatic.

"Oho. So, this is where the sword connects to the spine. The blade is certainly lodged in there, yes. As for its durability...it's nothing like your usual magic sword, I see. Is it because it was made specifically for this purpose? And what's this spell here?"

Eiworth poured a strange liquid on the sword while continuing his inspection of the body. He then stabbed something into the fanatic's eyeballs and drew blood from its neck.

"We're heading back, Eiworth."

"Oh, of course. There's nothing left for us here, after all. Did you find your dwarf friend? Is he all right?"

"He's not waking up."

"Come, let me see him."

Eiworth stored the corpse and Fran put Garrus down in front of him. She had hesitated at first, but in the end, she trusted his expertise.

"I see, I see..."

Eiworth inspected Garrus' tongue and eyelids to check the flow of his mana.

"It's the drugs," he said. "The stress has taken a toll on his psyche and is now affecting his body."

"Will he get better?" Fran asked.

"He's had quite the heavy dose, but it could be worse. He'll heal with time."

Eiworth was telling the truth, and Fran sighed with relief.

"How do we cure him?"

"Powerful Recovery spells," said Eiworth. "Or the alchemical equivalent. The drugs are powerful, but some medicines can heal its side effects. In fact, I can give you a hand. A drug-intoxicated dwarf is quite a rare specimen."

And this was where we refused!

Eiworth had the look of a wolf staring at fresh meat. I was concerned for Garrus' safety. He might not even come out in one piece!

"No thanks," Fran said.

"Hunh. Are you sure?"

"Hm."

"Come now, I can heal him here and now, if you'll let me," said Eiworth.

"We'll manage."

"Hrm..."

Fran had the same thought as me, but Eiworth just looked confused. Was he oblivious to what people thought of him?

What should we do now?

We needed to take Garrus somewhere safe to patch him up, but where?

Fran, let's go to the Adventurer's Guild. It's not too far, and they can heal and protect him.

"Hm. We're going to the Adventurer's Guild."

Eiworth nodded. "Yes, that's a good choice. It's not like you can hand him over to the Thieves' Guild, after all."

For once, we were in agreement. I thought for sure that Eiworth would insist we hand Garrus over to the Thieves' Guild.

"Let's drop off the dwarf quickly so we can head to the next battle," said Eiworth. "I would like to observe these things in action."

I guess he just wanted to sate his curiosity about the Fanatix replicas. If anything, I was surprised he didn't just bolt off on his own. It seemed like that would be more his style. Still, the thought of leaving Eiworth alone scared me a bit. We should probably keep an eye on him.

"And an Evolved Black Cat," he mused. "The rarest specimen of them all."

Eiworth gave Fran the same look—like he'd spotted a worthy test subject.

Fran, don't let your guard down around him.
Of course.

Fran wasn't going to relax around Eiworth, so we should be okay. Her animal instincts probably registered his gaze on her.

We left the way we came in, through the giant hole in the ground, picked up Face, and headed for the Adventurer's Guild. The city-wide tumult showed no signs of stopping. If anything, the chaos was spreading to the common and entertainment districts. Merchants and travelers were rushing to the city gates to escape.

"This looks bad." Face said. "People are trying to get away, but they might end up adding to the chaos."

He looked worried, and I didn't blame him. Fights were breaking out all over the city, loud explosions rang out continually, and to top it all off, there was a mysterious light shining from the noble district. There was also an immense mana coming from the direction of the palace. It was almost on the level of Marquis Aschtner's mana. Had the real Fanatix finally been unleashed?

Even with Face's guidance, we couldn't avoid running into more fanatics. Fortunately, they were easy to take out from a distance with a single Telekinetic Catapult. With their minds gone, they were barely even a threat.

"Let me have a turn!" Eiworth complained.

Fran groaned. "No one's stopping you."

She was definitely tired of the old man's antics, but Eiworth didn't seem to notice her ire. He jumped joyfully onto the frontlines.

"Ha ha! There are still things I wish to try."

He was wearing an evil grin, a far cry from the stony look on his face when we first met him. Eiworth took out another potion, but instead of throwing it at the enemy, he took it himself. The potion probably powered him up because he instantly leapt into close combat.

"..."

"Aah, I see! So you can nullify all mana—be it potion, skill, or physical enhancements!"

"..."

"Let's see how you handle this!"

Eiworth chucked another potion at the advancing fanatic, even while throwing his own fist at him. His timing was perfect. If the enemy dodged the potion, he would eat Eiworth's fist. Break the potion bottle, and he'd have to nullify its effects, exhausting his mana. Either way, Eiworth won.

We watched as the fanatic swung at the potion and shattered it—drenching himself with its contents. It was little more than water at this point, but the effects would be fatal. The fanatic had exhausted his mana nullifying the potion, and Eiworth froze him immediately. In an instant, the fight came to a pitiful end.

He's pretty good, said Fran.

Yeah. He has a lot of experience backing him up.

Hm. The only problem is there's no telling what he'll do.

Eiworth's fighting style seemed to be a mixture of magic, close combat, and potions. He lacked any obvious weaknesses, and that would make him a threat if we ever had to fight him. Fran watched carefully, trying to figure out how to beat him, just in case he turned on us—and Eiworth's lack of moral compass made that a frightening possibility.

We could probably deal with his spells and physique, I said. *But we know nothing about potions...*

They're strong.

You can say that again.

As Fran considered her anti-Eiworth tactics, we reached the Adventurer's Guild to find a war being waged in front of it. I guess that made sense, since the Adventurer's Guild was one of the greatest threats to the marquis' plan.

There were about fifty hostiles, including twenty soldiers with Fanatix replicas in their backs. There were ogre-like monsters with them too, standing two meters tall. Identifying one revealed that it was a Greater Flesh Golem, a necromantically formed creature made from the corpses of humans and monsters. It had low agility, but more than enough strength to make up for it. It was also very robust and could regenerate itself. With the mana-nullifying fanatics around, that was definitely a threat. If nothing else, they were giving the knights and adventurers hell.

There were about a hundred adventurers on the field—over a hundred and fifty including the ones that had been knocked out. Erianthe and Colbert were here too, but they were in a league of their own. Still, some of the other adventurers could keep up with them. In particular, I noticed the five insectoid halflings in matching armor. They were coordinating their attacks, so they must've been in the same party.

Must be the mercenaries Erianthe mentioned. Feeler and Shell, was it?

They certainly looked the part—with feelers coming out of their heads and parts of their body protected by shells. From what I could tell, there was a lobster, a grasshopper, a clam, a mayfly, and a bull ant. Of course, the mana nullification was keeping them from using their full powers, but they still fought like they could take down ten Greater Flesh Golems or more. Their fundamentals and experience were that good.

Teacher, over there.

Fran pointed at Stellia. She was surrounded by enemies.

We'll regroup with Erianthe after we save her.

"Hm!"

I fired a volley of spells at the fanatics. Of course, the spells were all nullified, but they should have drained the fanatics of mana. Fran leapt into the fray and cut them all down. The other adventurers were having so much difficulty dispatching their own fanatics that they stared at her in shock. Especially since she did it all while carrying Garrus. He wasn't that heavy, but the adventurers expected it to hinder her movement, at least. But Stellia only nodded.

"Nice going, Black Lightning! How'd you do that?"

Fran explained how to kill the fanatics, but Stellia looked concerned. Most people didn't have an infinite supply of potions and couldn't fire a volley of spells whenever they pleased.

"I suppose we could gather all the potions we can find," Stellia said. "Still, that's useful information. Now help us clear the road, would you?"

"Hm," said Fran. "But what about the rest of the city?"

"Don't you worry. The high ranks are taking care of it."

It seemed like adventurers were already dispatched throughout the city.

"Is that Garrus over your shoulder?" Stellia asked.

"Hm. He's still unconscious, though. Can you take care of him?"

"You got it. I won't let those bastards lay a finger on him. You take care of everyone else though, got it?"

"Got it. I'll take out the enemy."

Fran handed Garrus over to Stellia and covered them until they were safely inside the guild. Then we got ready for battle. Eiworth had caught up to us too.

"The sooner we do this, the better," he said. "Gods know how long those meat shields will last."

You can't just call those adventurers meat shields!

A number of them overheard his remark, but Erianthe soon called them off.

"Stop! This is no time for bickering!"

Erianthe must know all about Eiworth, both his powers *and* his personality. If anyone attacked him, they'd be done for before they knew what hit them. The adventurers glared daggers at Eiworth, but he ignored them—staring at the Fanatix replicas with deep interest instead.

"Save the meat golems for later. We need to thin out the swords first."

"I know."

Fran jumped into battle.

"Awaken."

We didn't know what to expect, so we saved Flashing Thunderclap for now. Not that we could use it, even if we needed to. Fran was still too exhausted. Still, a simple Awaken would be enough for now. The battlefield was chaotic, but it was easy enough to identify our enemies thanks to the swords in their backs. We just needed to sneak up behind them and take them out in one swing. We imbued our attacks with magic, just in case they were protected by barriers.

"Huh? What's that kid doing here? Whoa!"

"What's with the shadows?!"

The other adventurers were shocked at Fran's sudden arrival, but she had no time to entertain their questions and disappeared as quickly as she arrived. We could hear explosions and screaming in the distance. Eiworth must've been hustling too.

"Haaa!"

Colbert and Erianthe helped, and the mercenaries drew the enemy's attention away from us. That made our job a lot easier. Fifteen minutes later, the street was cleared of replicas. I fired a Kanna Kamuy at the last one, trying to find out how much mana it could nullify.

Yeah...I probably should've gone with a Thor's Hammer.

"Hm."

But a spell of Kanna Kamuy's caliber couldn't be so easily nullified. Its power output was lower, but it was still powerful enough to blow the fanatics to smithereens and leave a crater in front of the guild. The shock wave sent adventurers and Greater Flesh Golems flying.

Definitely too much.

"At least it didn't get deleted," said Fran.

Still, I was glad that the nullification absorbed some of the mana. The effects of a full-power Kanna Kamuy would've been disastrous.

I could feel the gaze of the other adventurers on us and wondered if they were upset at the giant hole in front of their guild. Even Eiworth was staring at Gran. Fortunately, the remaining flesh golems soon got their attention, and everyone got back to business. I guess it wasn't such a good idea to use a grand spell in front of the founder of the Mages' Guild.

Let's get some golems for ourselves.

"Hm!"

Now that the fanatics were gone, we could exterminate the Greater Flesh Golems. They were strong, but ultimately no match for us. We could even take it easy, watching how everyone else was doing. I was particularly interested in Colbert and Erianthe, since we'd been too occupied to watch them back in the Aschtner mansion.

Colbert fought like a regular martial artist. Losing the Dimitris Combat Arts really did a number on his offense. Now he wasn't as strong as he used to be and had to take down the flesh golems with repeated blows. However, he was stronger now that his strength was no longer sealed away. Despite losing his Dimitris style, he kept the fruits of his hard training. He would probably get stronger in the future as well.

Meanwhile, contrary to her appearance, Erianthe was a straight-up power fighter. She swung her giant sword at the flesh golems like she was simply taking out some everyday frustrations on them. The greatsword she'd brought to the Aschtner mansion was broken by a fanatic in Godsword Release, and the one she wielded now was much larger, at least twice its size. And yet, Erianthe didn't seem to mind the added weight at all. She must be packing a lot of power in her small frame.

"Aha ha ha ha! Eat this! And this!"

I thought the insectoid halfling didn't have feelers, but they were apparently hidden in her hair. The thick antennae peeked out of her disheveled purple hair and were long enough to be mistaken for horns. Now that I thought about it, her hair wasn't usually purple. Did it change color when she was fighting? It was purple back at the marquis' mansion too. I made a note to ask her later.

While she was fighting, Erianthe used her arachnid heritage to weave threads in battle. She shot webbing from her wrists to bind her enemies, much like a certain friendly neighborhood arachnid from another land. After that, she charged in, cackling wildly as she slammed down her greatsword. She looked like the very picture of a berserker, cutting up a golem's limbs with a single swing.

Let's leave her to her business.

The five insectoid mercenaries were still fighting together, and each one was strong on their own to boot. They were nothing like the mercenaries I'd seen before.

Who knew there were strong mercs?

Hm.

Of course, there *were* strong mercenaries out there, but my experience with the profession really called that into question from time to time. The stronger ones were usually found on the battlefield. Since we normally ran into mercenaries in other places, it was no wonder that the ones we had seen were weak.

The lobster halfling punched a flesh golem right in front of Fran. He must be the hot-blooded leader since he was the one issuing orders. I figured he must be the spiny variant. Parts of his face and right hand were covered with a smooth red shell, while his hand was covered in spikes, like a giant meat tenderizer. He made a motion with his fist, casting a Water spell on a flesh golem to finish it off.

The grasshopper halfling's legs were *huge*. While the upper half of his body looked handsome and young, his legs was thick as tree trunks. He wore baggy pants to compensate, but his bulging legs made them look skintight.

"I'll break you to pieces!"

His lower body strength was incredible. A single kick made the one-ton golem rise off the ground. His movements flowed like a taekwondo or capoeira practitioner, so most of his strength must come from his legs.

The mayfly halfling was a lancer. Her thin wings didn't look like they could help her to fly, but she could use them to make sudden turns. Her slim body quickly navigated the battlefield, making her a tricky opponent to fight. On top of that, the sleepy expression on her face made her all the harder to read. Her strengths weren't much against mindless meat golems, but in a duel, she would be a force to be reckoned with.

The bull ant halfling looked a lot like an ordinary human, but with feelers and bug eyes. Standing at 160 centimeters tall, the innocent-looking girl seemed out of place on a battlefield. However, her two axes put that assumption to rest. She somersaulted round the battle with an axe in each hand, making quick work of the golems. She could also blind her enemies by shooting poison out of her mouth. The bull ant halfling was as powerful as she was agile.

Finally, there was the clam halfling. He certainly *looked* like a shellfish, but I guess they were considered insectoids in this world. Either way, he was a big guy, and it seemed like he had a big heart to go with it. This one wasn't a fighter, but a mage utilizing Illusion spells. He reminded me of the *Shen,* a mythical clam monster from my world. His back and shoulders were armored with shell, making him much tougher than your average spellcaster. A flesh golem swung at him, and curled up to take the hit. I guess this mage was also the tank of the party, which was kind of strange.

Meanwhile, Fran was frustrated at having to fight without mana, and overkilled another flesh golem to vent her annoyance.

"Haaaa!"

She chopped off its limbs and split its head with a Pressurized Quickdraw. It must've felt amazing not to be restrained. Of course, given her current state of exhaustion, this was all she could do. Eiworth wasn't the only one hustling on the battlefield. This catgirl was doing the same. The only difference was, Fran's battle fury actually increased morale.

"Come on! We can't lose to the little beastgirl!"

"Especially not when we're getting paid by the boatload!"

"Yeah!"

The adventurers and insect rangers were completely motivated now. I mean, the insectoids were more like cyborgs, but there were five of them! They were the Hardhitting Hardshell Insect Rangers! Red Lobster, Green Grasshopper, White Mayfly, Black Bull Ant. The clam was mostly gray, but clams came from the sea, so he could be considered blue...but since he was the nice guy of the group, he could be yellow too. Either way, they were the perfect embodiment of the ranger spirit!

Suddenly, I felt a magical response coming from the middle of the road, and a huge cloud of purple gas covered the street and the buildings. That wasn't something you wanted in your body.

Fran, don't breathe it in! Danger Sense is going crazy!
Hm!

I quickly covered us with a wind barrier to protect Fran from the poison, while the insect rangers huddled behind the mayfly's Wind spell and the lobster's Water spell. When the fog cleared, Greater Flesh Golems and adventurers alike were lying on the ground twitching. In the midst of it all, an old man laughed.

"Hah! I knew paralysis would work on these golems! They're made of human flesh, after all."

Eiworth had cast a deadly Venom spell on our enemies and allies alike.

"Don't worry. The poison has no lasting side effects. I'll cure you all when we're done. If you're still on your feet, focus on killing these meat bags."

"That old bastard...!"

"Guildmaster, we should really take care of the golems first!"

Erianthe and Colbert were still standing. Erianthe was about to give Eiworth a piece of her mind, but Colbert held her back.

Still, Eiworth had a point. The humans were pretty much unharmed, and now we had an opening to kill the golems. The mercenaries were visibly angry at his actions, but they still heeded his words. Unethical as the old man was, they couldn't waste this opportunity. All the same, only someone who didn't care about human rights could pull off a tactic like that. That was Eiworth to a tee.

I sure wouldn't be able to do something like that.

"Killing them one by one is a waste of time, don't you think?"

There was only one person who agreed with him.

Fran nodded. "I see."

Fran? Why are you impressed? We are not *doing something like that, got it? No way!*

SIDE: URSLARS

"Been a long time since I've been to Jillbird."

"Gods, you're huge, mister. You an ogrekin?"

"You guessed it."

I watched the harbor on the horizon as the sailor talked to me. He seemed friendly and looked at me with great interest. People usually kept a safe distance away from me, so it was quite the new sensation. There weren't many ogrekin in this continent, so rumors of my arrival would probably spread immediately.

"Business or pleasure?" the sailor asked.

"Can't say it's business, exactly..."

If anything, I made the crossing from Chrome to Jillbird on something closer to a whim.

"Call it a hunch."

"A hunch?" The sailor tilted his head. "Really?"

That was fair enough. People didn't usually cross oceans on a hunch.

It sounded like a throwaway answer, but I was telling the truth. My Class Skill, Premonition, enhanced my intuition and instinct. It allowed me to judge whether someone was lying and let me sense traps and hidden enemies in dungeons. It wasn't infallible, but it had saved my life many times. And now, my intuition pointed me in the direction of Jillbird.

Murelia, a Fiend, probably had something to do with it. When she died, she said she wanted us to save a boy called Romeo. And she wasn't lying, I knew that for sure. I also sensed a deep sadness from a man called Theraclede. He was cruel, but his sadness was real. Back then, I still didn't know why...

I only understood later, when I heard that Theraclede had kidnapped Romeo. I didn't know why he pretended to betray Murelia, but he was on her side until the very end. So, of course, Theraclede would carry out her last will and testament.

But even then, it took a while to work out where he

would take the child. Murelia researched orphanages before she died, and one of the candidates was in the city of Bulbola. Mea and the others found that out after looking through Murelia's belongings, so I knew it was true.

There really wasn't much of a point in my following the trail. I didn't know whether I wanted to rescue Romeo or just have a rematch with Theraclede, but after letting my feet take me where they wanted to go, I found myself on a boat headed for Jillbird.

"It feels like I'm on a wild goose chase..."

I got off the boat and asked around for the location of the orphanage. It was pretty famous in town, especially after an A-Rank became its chief patron. Once there, I asked a modest-looking woman about Romeo, but apparently he was no longer here.

"Theraclede took him away..."

I could just let the whole thing end here, but...

"Something stinks."

The whole thing just didn't sit well with me. So, instead of forgetting about the whole incident, it took up my full attention. Where had Theraclede gone?

Besides, I couldn't just give up, not after coming all the way across the ocean. I at least wanted to see Theraclede and the boy for myself.

"So, where to next?"

Theraclede was a wanted criminal across the whole world, so bringing a child along would only cause him trouble. If nothing else, Romeo would make it difficult for Theraclede to run away in a hurry. Still, there *was* a place where fugitives could live in relative ease. A safe haven for criminals around the world. Somewhere where a strong man like Theraclede could make a living quite easily.

"Goldicia. Where the past remains buried for the strong..."

People in Goldicia hired anyone, no questions asked, as long as you helped them meet their daily quota. They weren't going to lose out on someone strong because of something as meaningless as their past actions.

"Which means I'll have to go east to get a boat to Goldicia."

That was on the other side of Jillbird, but it gave me the opportunity to stop by Granzell's capital.

"Don't think I've ever been there before. I normally just keep going on to Alessa."

The capital was majestic. I'd never seen so many ramparts in all my long years. It was hard to find the right place to build a capital city. The surrounding areas must be clear of powerful monsters and their spawn points, the environment had to be stable, it needed to be easy to get to, and there also had to be a water source. Ticking off all these boxes was difficult. Finding a spot free of strong monsters around was especially tough. You just couldn't build a city where dragons and giants kept spawning nearby, and even if you did, it probably wouldn't last very long.

In that respect, Granzell's capital was in the perfect spot. Only small and medium-sized monsters spawned in the area, and they could be easily dispatched by a team of adventurers and knights. Even if a big monster strayed into the region, the capital's manatek weapons would make quick work of it while its powerful barriers kept the city safe. Even a country as big as Granzell had difficulty gathering all of its strong fighters in one place. If they happened to hang around for a while, great. But countries last for hundreds of years, so defense which relied on numbers and equipment was much more reliable. The capital was the center of a country's civilization, after all.

"Didn't think there would be riots here..."

As I looked for information on Theraclede, a sudden explosion shook the city. I left the bar where I was asking questions and stepped outside. Pillars of fire shot up all over the city. This was no ordinary brawl. I didn't know if it was a coup, but I spotted humans fighting with each other. The capital was impregnable from the outside, but on the inside, it was as vulnerable as any other city.

Either way, this riot was *huge.* I figured that I probably shouldn't pick sides as things would get messy if I intervened. But as I was thinking about what to do, I was attacked by freaks with swords in their backs. They were pretty strong, and they could nullify magic too. I didn't sense any emotion or reason within them. I didn't even know who they were, but I couldn't let them run amok here.

The Adventurer's Guild had several branches in the capital, and they told me that a marquis was staging a coup. The people with swords in their backs were his men, and their guildmaster had already enlisted elites to help.

"Don't suppose I can just let things be."

I didn't know whether or not the capital was fortunate to have me here, but I wanted to make sure that Fran was okay. That was a good trade. My investigation of Theraclede might have ended in a dead end, but at least I knew that Fran was in town. Apparently, she stood out here as much as anywhere else. For now, I would see what I could learn at the palace, where the knights were focusing their efforts.

I'll take care of their marquis problem if I have to.

I had a lot of fight left in me after Fran and the others calmed me down, so I wouldn't have to worry about going berserk for a while.

Evidently, I was being too optimistic.

By the time I got to the palace, a girl was destroying the knight brigade. She was a drake with blue scales on her body, and she was emitting enough mana to rival my own. I didn't know what she was doing, but if she wanted to level the capital, she could do it in a minute or so. I had to intervene. Fran and Teacher would be in danger if I didn't.

So, I greeted the bigwigs talking about Dimitris, then launched myself into an attack on the drake girl. It didn't do much damage, so I started thinking I'd have to get serious here.

"But how long can I last?"

If I went berserk in the middle of the fight, then things would go from bad to worse. That was a genuine threat when I was fighting an enemy this powerful. Buying time here was not an option. I had to end this quick. The knights were ordering people to evacuate, so I guess they were paying attention to me. Still, their commander had more balls than I thought.

"Hey, get everyone out of here!" I said. "You don't wanna get caught in the crossfire when I start fighting!"

"Wh-who are you...?"

"The name's Urslars. Adventurer. You may know me as Friendly Fire Urslars."

The commander's face paled. "All knights, evacuate the citizens and fall back! Retreat to the palace immediately!"

"Sir!"

He gave the order as soon as he heard my name. Smart guy. That should make it easier for me to take care of this.

"You ever heard of an adventurer called the Black Lightning Princess?" I asked.

"You are acquainted with Fran, Sir Urslars?"

Jackpot.

"I am. Where is she now?"

"She is investigating Marquis Aschtner's mansion."

"Is that far from here?"

"Quite."

Great. That meant I wouldn't have to worry about hurting her either. I still winced at the thought of accidentally killing acquaintances. My conscience kept quiet for all the rest though.

"You guys better split before you get hit!"

Now I can go all out. I haven't had the chance to let loose in a long time.

"Haaaa! Godsword Release!"

At my command, Gaia transformed. The immense mana sent chills down my spine as the doors holding back the Godsword's power were blown wide open.

Gaia allowed its user to use Land Magic. I had its entire arsenal of spells at my beck and call now that it was unleashed. I could even borrow mana and fire off grand spells. No wonder people called me a weapon.

"Gravity Prison!"

"Gaah!"

And yet the girl easily broke out of my spell. She must have a lot of Magic Resistance. Binding spells wouldn't do much good here. This was going to turn into a slugfest.

"Hey, ugly!"

Well, that was a surprise. The girl might look like she'd lost all control, but she could still talk. Still, something wasn't right. She seemed to be speaking with the voice of a man. All of that was fine by me. More talking meant more time for people to get away.

"What?"

"That's a Godsword you have there, isn't it? A real Godsword, not like the fake one the Black Cat brat has!"

"Black Cat?" I said. "Are you talking about Fran?"

"If we have your Godsword..."

"Hey!"

"If we have more Godswords..."

She could talk, but she was too crazed to have a proper conversation. As she mumbled, the girl's sword emanated wicked mana. Was she being controlled by it? Was her sword an Intelligent Weapon like Teacher? Teacher seemed human enough, but this thing was completely insane. Whatever it was, it wasn't a good sword, that was for sure.

"Who are you?" I asked.

"I don't know! That's what I wanna find out! But I do know one thing... We can go back to normal with that Godsword!" The broken sword was *definitely* talking through the girl. "Hand it over!"

I had its attention now, and that worked out just fine. It wasn't as likely to run away now.

"Time to get serious."

I couldn't sense anyone else in the vicinity. There were still people in the palace, but it was better to destroy the noble district than the common one. At least the nobles could afford to rebuild the area their houses.

"We need it to fix us!" said the girl.

"I'm not attached to this thing, but you're not getting it!"

"Then I'll kill you and take it from your corpse!"

"Bring it on!"

We started the fight in high gear, trading blows that leveled mansions in a single swing. Our surroundings were reduced to ruins in less than a minute. Roads turned into rubble and large holes were gouged in the ground. Even then, both of us were still holding back. We would feint to bait a powerful attack, but even if it landed, the fight went on. Arms were bent, legs were broken, our bodies were riddled with holes. But the wounds healed, and our weapons kept clashing.

"Why can't I control you?!" cried the girl.

"Control me?"

Apparently, the enemy had some kind of mind control power. That wouldn't work on me. I was already under the terrible influence of Mad Ogre Form. So long as you couldn't surpass that awful Skill, you would be hard-pressed to control me.

"Yaaaah!"

"Aaargh!"

The cycle of attacking and healing repeated for a while, but the girl was beginning to panic. Even though it looked like we were evenly matched, she was at a disadvantage. She couldn't maintain this stalemate for long. Our abilities were even. She was better at regenerating her health, and I was better at controlling the battlefield. But the difference between our weapons was clear. I was wielding a Godsword, while the girl had some kind of broken magic sword.

Even if she could heal every hit I landed on her, she couldn't recover from a Godsword's damage so easily. It wasn't easy to tell, but she was getting exhausted. Her movements were getting slower—not by much, but enough to make a difference. The battle was beginning to turn in my favor. She was landing fewer hits, while I was landing more.

In an attempt to whittle me down, the girl took to the skies and pelted me with projectiles. But she overextended and got too close—either because she was desperate to steal my Godsword, or because she needed to cut me with her sword to control me. She must've been confident with her swordplay.

Under normal circumstances, the girl would've overwhelmed me with her superior Sword Mastery, but Gaia was too powerful for her. With its power unleased, it was imbued with a divine element, taking a chunk out of her life with every swing. Of course, I was feeling the pressure too. The last time I was up against an enemy like this, it was a lich, an A-Threat monster. But awareness was the first step to overcoming this kind of pressure, and I was plenty aware of that now.

"Aaargh!"

She's backing off!

But I wasn't going to let her get away now that she was at a disadvantage. I brought the Land Sword Gaia down to the earth and used its ability.

"Kiss of the Land!"

"Yaaaaargh!"

An area around a hundred meters in diameter was immediately flattened and driven down by an invisible force. This was no Land spell—this was the power of Gaia itself. The girl slammed into the ground, yanked by the force of the land. Gravity pushed her down hard into the ground.

Was that too much?

My surroundings were completely flattened, including the walls protecting those inside the castle. But the safety of the capital was at stake here, so I did what I had to.

"Land's Embrace!"

The flattening focused in on one spot, creating a cage of gravity around the girl and perfectly constricting her. Her mouth opened in a silent scream. This combo would've killed an earth dragon in an instant. Enduring it was commendable, but teleporting away was the only way to escape.

The girl screamed before I could deal the final blow.

"GODSWORD RELEASE!"

"Dammit!"

She broke free of the gravitational cage, and the mana coming off of her began to rival Gaia's. I hadn't needed to be on my toes like this in a while.

"'Godsword Release'?"

That's what I'd heard, anyway. Was that sword of hers a Godsword? It looked broken, but maybe it was a discarded one, like Teacher.

I knew a thing or two about Godswords since I'd been acquainted with Aristea for so long. There were six discarded ones that I knew of. Cherubim, Meltdown, Judgment were the three that the gods had ordered to be destroyed, so it couldn't be any of these three. But it *had* to be a Godsword. If it only looked like one, as Teacher did, it wouldn't have this much power. That meant it was probably destroyed in an accident or battle. It could only be Holy Order, Fanatix, or El Dorado.

As I pondered the Godsword's identity, a shrill voice broke out.

"That's it! You're dead, asshole! Forty years I slaved away for this!"

"Tell that to someone who cares!" I shouted back.

"I chipped off bits of myself and melted them down to forge replicas. Now we have a dragon maiden whose bloodline possesses Shinryu Form. And just when everything's lined up, *you* showed up to ruin it all!"

The sword was wailing in frustration. Despite unleashing its powers, it was still broken. However, its guard had grown larger—forming a gauntlet that now covered the girl's arm up to her elbow. It was etched with countless human faces, but one stood out. It looked like a man's head and it seemed to represent the sword's core. It was the same size as an adult male and moved like one too. Even its expressions were human.

"So, you're the one behind this mess?" I asked.

The sword cackled. "That's right! We got Aschtner to do our dirty work! Not that it worked out!"

"What do you want?"

"Phyllius' Godsword, Diablos! I was going to take control of the king and order an invasion of Phyllius, until you came along!"

"To fix you...?" I asked, looking at Gaia.

If this sword wanted Gaia to repair itself, then it probably wanted Diablos for the same reason.

"Yes!" the sword screamed. "I need Godswords made of Orichalcos, and Diablos was also made by Dionis! Like us! It will be a perfect match!"

That confirmed my suspicions. This was definitely Fanatix, the Sword of Mad Faith. It had lost most of its power when it was defeated by Holy Order, but it managed to escape complete destruction. Apparently, it had been plotting to repair itself ever since, and it didn't care how much blood was shed as long as it could be made whole again.

But the thing that shocked me most was the fact that

it had a mind of its own. Still, meeting Teacher softened the blow somewhat.

"It's all your fault... I'll kill you, even if I have to break myself to do it! I'll kill *everyone* in this city! You're all dead!"

The sword's broken blade began disintegrating. Was Godsword Release taking its toll on it? At this rate, it was only a matter of time before Fanatix destroyed itself. The full force of its own power was too great for the broken Godsword.

"Come at me, you scrap metal!" I shouted.

"Gladly! You'll be the first to die!"

3

Blood on the Streets

WE MANAGED TO DEFEAT the flesh golems, thanks to Eiworth's reckless measures, but we weren't out of the woods just yet. Though the paralysis had long since worn off, there were still plenty of wounded.

Eiworth approached Fran, ignoring our injured allies.

"You cast a grand spell!" he said, as soon as she left her Awakened state. His eyes were gleaming, but I didn't sense an ounce of jealousy from him. He was far too inquisitive for that. "I didn't think you reached the pinnacle of Thunder Magic!"

"Hm."

"And you controlled it all by yourself," he mused. "Are you using any special equipment?"

"Trade secret."

"Please! I must know!"

For once, Eiworth clasped his hands and asked nicely. His curiosity was begging to be sated.

"No."

"Oh, all right," he groaned. "So how does it feel? How much mana do you use? How much effort do you put into controlling it? How much mana do you spend compared to a regular spell?"

Eiworth wasted no time with his interview, but Fran only gave him vague answers. Still, it wasn't like she was being evasive. Her vocabulary was just limited to words like 'a lot' and 'tons' when it came to describing things. Eiworth needed more precision than that, so after a while, he gave up. Just as well, since Fran was exhausted. She usually acted by her feelings, but the tiredness made her even more vague than usual. Someone who also operated the same way would probably understand her. Probably. In any case, that was all the conversation we could afford for now. There was still trouble afoot.

"Hrm?"

"Oh? Something's closing in on us. Was there a spell cast on the golems?"

Fran and Eiworth turned their attention to Main Street, where an unnatural amount of mana was forming. It was coming out of the defeated flesh golems and was probably set to trigger after they died. People started destroying their corpses, but it was too late. A giant magic circle hovered over Main Street. A bright glow lit up the area, and more mana swirled around. It concentrated further until it was on the level of a grand spell.

Fran tried destroying it, but her attacks were deflected by the sheer concentration of mana. The spell was past the point where we could stop it. I put up a powerful barrier, just as the circle glowed to its brightest point. I wish I could protect all the adventurers around me, but it was hopeless.

Huh?

But the explosion never came.

It's not an attack?

I thought the spell would raze everything around us, but everything was still standing. Instead, something strange appeared on top of the magic circle. It was…summoning something.

What is that thing?

"A coffin?" Fran muttered.

Actually, it's more like a sarcophagus if we're being precise…

A gigantic stone coffin fell onto Main Street. It was five meters tall and three meters wide. Back on Earth, this size coffin would've been reserved for nobility, but here, it could just be an ordinary coffin for the larger races. The sarcophagus stood upright and started emitting ominous mana. Whatever this was, it wasn't just for decoration.

"Is that a necromantic seal on its cover? I can feel something inside."

"There's something inside that thing?"

"Indeed. And the seal is keeping it there."

Was there an undead monster inside that box? Was this sarcophagus being used as intended by its summoner? If so, then the undead inside must be pretty big. Fran, Eiworth, and some of the stronger adventurers all readied their weapons, but the coffin got the drop on us. Its heavy lid fell on the ground with a thud, revealing its contents.

"What is it?" Fran asked.

"Looks like meat," Eiworth mused.

Either way, it's gross!

We couldn't tell what it was—all we saw was a salmon-pink mass, crammed into the coffin. It was slick and shiny like a mollusk, and the sight of it was enough to terrify the already tense adventurers.

Suddenly, something that looked like an eye blinked open. It was clouded over like a dead fish, but it was definitely glaring at us. Then, blood vessels pulsed all over its surface. This thing was a mass of flesh that had somehow been packed into the coffin.

"Aaaarrgh..."

The thing produced a low growl, which echoed down Main Street. It was emitting undead mana, and slowly wriggled itself free from the coffin using the two meat clubs hanging down its sides to pull itself out. The meat clubs had five meat sticks to grip the side of the coffin. These were its arms and fingers, of course.

"Aaaagh..."

A head poked out of the flesh lump, announcing itself to the world. It had two bulging eyeballs now, but no nose or mouth yet. Perhaps more organs would be revealed when the rest of its head came out of the meat bag.

Looks like we're in for some trouble.

This thing must be some kind of fail-safe in case the flesh golems were wiped out. In that case, there was no reason to wait around then. Seemingly, Eiworth had the same idea.

"Surely we don't need to wait for it to complete itself?" he asked. "Let's kill it before it is born."

"Hm."

Fran was in full agreement, and both of them started charging up their spells. The other adventurers followed suit. Fran and I were the first to fire a No-Cast spell.

"Flare Blast!"

Flare Blast!

It was a low-level Flame spell, but it was still powerful if you charged it enough. Highly effective against both the living and the undead. Our spell headed straight for the fleshy lump and...suddenly disappeared.

Mana nullification?!

"Hrm."

"All that mana gone in an instant!" Eiworth laughed. "Let's see how you handle this."

He fired off some spells of his own, despite knowing that they would likely get nullified too. Still, fighting a strong opponent was a research opportunity as far as this old man was concerned. Attacking his research subject was all part of the process.

"Frost Jail!"

A spell that would freeze its surroundings. It killed weaker opponents, while stronger ones would be frozen in place for a time. However, before it could reach the sarcophagus, this was nullified too. The other adventurers tried pelting it with more spells to no avail. This meat mass might also have a Fanatix replica stuck in it somewhere.

Finally, the creature made its full appearance. It looked like a skinless undead giant, standing four meters tall. Its salmon-pink skin was peeling off, and the sight was gruesome enough that some of the adventurers struggled to keep down their lunch. Apparently, the giant was actually a huge beastman.

"Aah, is that an elephant's trunk on its head?" Eiworth asked.

"Hm. It does look like an elephant beastman."

Large floppy ears, long trunk, sharp tusks. *Definitely an elephant head.* We saw some elephant beastmen back in the Beastman Nation, and that must be what this thing was made from. A pink elephant might sound like a cute fairy-tale creature, but this bipedal monster with his bulging veins came straight out of a nightmare.

Considering his head, and his size, I think he's Awakened.

The beastmen we'd met were about three meters tall with heads like a human. Apparently, Awakening increased their size and made their features more elephantine.

"Hm. He's Awakened."

"Really? And here I thought it was an ordinary undead. It must have been created through special means." Eiworth chuckled. "Very interesting!"

Is research the only thing you can think about?!

I was more worried about the undead elephantman having mana nullification abilities, but Eiworth wasn't the only one who got pumped up at the prospect of fighting a strong opponent.

"He looks strong."

Fran, not you too!

Considering how much Fran enjoyed battle, I guess her excitement was inevitable.

"OAAAAAAAAARGH!"

The undead elephant let out a roar laced with Intimidate. It sent fear down the spines of ordinary soldiers, but Fran and Eiworth simply shook their heads at the volume of it. The elephantman wasn't that much stronger than them and, even if he was, the difference in strength wasn't overwhelming. However, most of the other adventurers were frozen in fear, further reducing our numbers. Were Fran and Eiworth doomed to fight the undead elephant alone?

The elephantman looked around and opened his mouth. I braced for another roar, but he started talking instead.

"AAAAAH! Invaders! I won't let you have the capital! I will protect this kingdom!"

Apparently, he was intelligent enough to speak.

"He talked."

"You see this sometimes in specimens with gruesome grudges," said Eiworth.

"Invaders?" Fran said. "Us?"

"Don't think too much of it. It's just the grudge talking. It's being driven by the same grudges it had in its past life."

"UOOOOOH!"

The undead elephant turned its fury on us.

Here he comes!

"Ha ha ha! Don't get in my way, girl!"

"Worry about yourself!"

Fran and Eiworth split up to attack. I couldn't imagine Eiworth cooperating with anyone, and Fran wasn't really one for teamwork either, so it was better if they both attacked alone, at their own pace.

"Come on, boys!"

"On it!"

The insect rangers were still on their feet too. I expected nothing less from these top mercenaries.

"Colbert, evacuate the injured!"

"Got it!"

Erianthe and the others were helping the wounded up and away from the battlefield. Now we could focus on fighting.

"Let's try this to start!"

Eiworth threw several bottles at the elephantman. I didn't know what was in them, but the potions surely contained powerful magic. He wanted to exhaust the elephant's mana, the same way he'd done with the fanatic soldiers, but this time, the bottles were swept up in a whirlwind before they hit their target.

"DIIIIIIE!"

The potions hurtled toward us instead, moving at a deadly pace. They broke against a pavement, letting out a deadly poison gas.

"Ack!"

"My eyes!"

"I can't breathe...!"

Dammit, Eiworth!

A powerful wind spread the gas everywhere, and adventurers started dropping like flies. The elephantman must have realized what was in the bottles and decided to use them against us.

"Damn thing's smart for an undead golem!" Eiworth complained, firing off another spell. "Dangerous Play!"

The poison gathered up and snaked toward Eiworth like it had a mind of its own. That spell must have collected the poison in one spot so he could fire it again. While I watched, I healed up nearby adventurers. As capricious as Eiworth was, his strategy had worked against the greater flesh golems. Perhaps it would work here too.

But Eiworth's poison bomb was dissipated by the wind swirling around to protect the elephantman. Our foe had finer control of Wind Magic than I thought.

An elephant beastman who uses the wind...

What is it, Teacher?

Purple Wind Elephant was one of the Ten Ancestors, wasn't it?

So, you're saying that undead is Evolved?

Maybe.

The Ten Ancestors were the predecessors of the Ten Tribes, the strongest of the beastmen. Fran and her tribe could Evolve into Black Sky Tigers. The Beast King and Mea were Golden Fire Lions. The Purple Wind Elephant was one of the Ten too. Awakened, he could probably rival Fran's strength, and he had mana nullification to boot.

Don't let your guard down! I don't think he's fighting at full force yet!

"Hm!"

Fran nodded, circling the undead elephant and casting various elemental spells to try and penetrate his defenses. Unfortunately, most of them were blown away by the wind, and what few spells made it through were nullified.

It's like having a steel wall on top of a steel wall!

"*BAROOOO!*"

The pachyderm blew his trunk. He was occupied with Eiworth before, but now Fran had his attention. Apparently, he judged her to be more dangerous.

He's so fast!

"Urgh...!"

Fran barely dodged the elephant's charge. One second more and she would've been gored by his tusks. This thing was more agile than he looked. He didn't even need to crouch before he started sprinting at us. In fact, his posture was mostly upright. He must be accelerating himself with the wind and cutting down on air resistance. Either way, the sight of his gigantic body streaking toward us was ridiculous. We had to be careful here.

Back off, Fran! Gain some distance!

"Hm!"

Getting into a melee with this thing was a bad idea, but we didn't exactly have the specs for long-range combat either. I thought the greater distance might help us, but spells weren't the elephantman's only ranged option.

"BAHROOOMP!"

Wind Wall!

"Was that a Wind spell?"

No! He compressed wind in his trunk and fired it at us!

The elephant's trunk shot like a cannon as it extended toward us. Its pressurized air took out my Wind Wall in a single shot. It managed to throw off the shot's trajectory, but Fran would've been gravely injured if it had gone through. The wind cannonball broke through several walls before exploding a house twenty meters away.

Teacher, we have to get closer!

That's not a good idea...!

He's going to shoot another wind shot if we stay at this range! People might die!

Our surroundings were even more of a mess after the elephant started firing his wind cannon. But as exhausted as Fran was, she didn't have a chance against one of the Ten Tribes.

I'm going in. Set a barrier for me.

Aaah, fine! You have to focus on dodging though, got it?

Okay!

But someone else got to the pachyderm before she did.

"Don't forget about us!"

"Actually, it would help me a lot if you did!"

The insect rangers had arrived. They dropped into a battle formation with the armored lobster at the forefront.

Fran, they might be able to handle the elephantman! Let's switch to support.

Hm.

We cast support spells on the insect halflings after changing our strategy. Most of it was to bolster their defenses. The lobster realized this and nodded his head toward us. The others thanked us too. That would be enough to let them know our plan.

"Let's not disappoint the young lady!"

"*YEAH!*"

Erianthe's trusty mercenaries leapt into action with deadly precision.

"Yaaaaah!"

Their lobster leader took point and attacked the enemy first. A quick Identify revealed his name as Robin. His natural defense from his red shell and elegant movement allowed him to take the elephantman head-on.

The undead elephant wasn't equipped with any weapons, but his physical prowess, trunk, and tusks were enough to make him a threat in close combat.

Even so, Robin handled himself well. Not a single attack had landed on him so far. He weaved through the undead's swings and delivered a one-two punch right into his knee—all while evading the trunk that was coming at him from behind. Robin blocked the elephant's tusks with his hard shell and landed another set of jabs into his leg. His fighting style wasn't flashy, but it was very effective.

Robin's teammates weren't just standing around, either. Each had their role against a physically large opponent.

Hobbes, the grasshopper, expanded his legs and jumped behind the elephantman. Robin was keeping him occupied so he could kick his enemy from the sides and the rear. His bulging legs looked heavy, but they packed a ton of speed and power. One jump was all Hobbes needed to get behind the enemy. There was a loud crack every time he jumped, but he was doing it on purpose. Though it announced his position, the noise was loud enough to break the enemy's concentration.

"You're so slow! You can't catch me with that speed!"

"Get back here you fly!"

"I'm a grasshopper, actually!"

"Gaaaaargh!"

Hobbes kept harassing the undead elephant while staying out of his clutches. His movements were impressive, but he could only move like that thanks to the aid of his party members.

"...Gotcha."

Effie the mayfly murmured aloud as she stabbed the elephantman with her spear. She specialized in tricky movements and spearplay, but apparently she had another trick up her sleeve. I didn't notice her at all until she made her attack. She must be excellent at stealth too.

While her attack didn't do much damage, the back attack forced the elephantman to stop attacking Hobbes to address her.

"Raaaargh!"

"So dumb."

Effie jumped back with her wings while mocking her undead foe.

"Get back here!"

He extended his trunk toward her, but an axe stopped his attack short.

"And don't forget me! WHAM!"

It was Ann the bull ant. Between Robin, Hobbes, and Effie, the elephantman was completely defenseless. Ann took advantage of the situation by concealing herself before attacking. She landed on the ground and used her dual axes to work on the elephantman's legs. Identify revealed that she didn't have any Stealth Skills. Shingen the clam probably helped her with that.

Ann's axes tore chunks of flesh off of the undead and broke his knee. It was the same knee Robin had been working on from the start. The mercenaries made a coordinated effort to focus on the same body part. The elephantman was already regenerating, but he couldn't move until then. This was a huge opening. However, the mercs huddled into a defensive position. Shingen took point here, using his big body to protect his allies.

Just then, the undead elephant released powerful gusts of wind.

"*BAHROOOOOO!*"

The move prevented the mercs from exploiting the opening. I was impressed that they could stop their attacks and immediately go on the defensive. Maybe their instincts and intuition were better because of their insectoid blood. All of them had the Intuition Skill as well. Back in Ulmutt, Elza managed to sense that I Identified him with Intuition.

Wait, does that mean they sensed me Identifying them? Maybe I should apologize later.

Teacher?

I-it's nothing. Did you see that?

Hm. His mana dropped when he started healing himself.

Apparently, he's not as good at regenerating as he is at attacking.

I didn't know whether mana nullification used up the elephant's mana. It must be hidden really well because I couldn't even sense its presence.

All I knew was, the mana surrounding the elephant-man decreased when he healed himself. For some reason, attacking and mana nullification didn't use up much mana for him, but regeneration did. Forcing him to keep healing himself might be the key to this battle.

"What should we do?"

Hmm.

Melee was our only option since all our spells would just be nullified. But getting up close with that thing? The elephantman was now on the counterattack, charging toward the insect rangers at a great speed. The charge was enough to blow away Robin and Shingen. Shingen managed to block it with his back, but the attack still took away half his stamina.

A melee attack was a bad idea, but Fran was determined to get in.

"I'm going."

I knew that look in her eyes. There was nothing that could stop her when she was like this. They'd only fought together for a few moments, but Fran considered the insect rangers her friends now. And she wasn't going to stand by and let her friends remain in danger.

All right! I'll handle defense!

"Hm! Haaa!"

Fran nodded and dashed in at the first opportunity she got.

She drew the elephant's attention away from the insect rangers by attacking him from behind. The undead's eyes were filled with hatred and disgust when he saw that a small black cat girl was the one cutting him.

"*DIIIIIIE!*"

"Too slow."

Watch out for the wind!

The elephantman kicked Fran and she avoided it easily, but that was exactly what he wanted. A wind spear came right at her afterward. It wasn't very powerful, but Fran was wide open and had no way of defending herself. The undead's brains hadn't rotted away, that was for sure. Fran managed to dodge both the wind spear and the elephant's trunk before using a Pressurized Quickdraw on his knee... but my blade couldn't land on the elephantman.

"Oooorgh!"

The winds again!

So hard!

The layers of wind on top of the undead's skin were so dense that I couldn't penetrate them. Fran pushed and strained, but it was no use. The elephantman must have known what she was going to do and switched to defense. The winds weren't this thick at the beginning of the battle.

Get back!

"Ah!"

The trunk came after her again. She jumped to the side as it came plunging down on her from above. It smashed right into the ground, leaving a hole behind. The trunk then came after Fran like a whip with unpredictable angles.

How flexible could a trunk be?!

The elephantman's trunk snaked around her like an anaconda. But Fran managed to avoid all of it.

This is nothing compared to Amanda's whip.

Of course!

The sparring match we had with her back in Alessa was finally paying dividends. The A-Rank's whip was much livelier than this trunk. Fran managed to strike at it a couple times, but it was covered in tough muscle.

"Hrm."

Fran grunted, annoyed. She knew that she lacked power because she wasn't Awakened. She then collected herself and jumped back from the elephantman.

I'm sensing a lot of mana from Eiworth!

"Hm!"

Eiworth had been concealing his presence so far and we only detected the mana he was charging up. I thought he had been content to observe Fran and the others fight, but the old man wasn't out just yet.

He cast his spell just as Fran moved away—then again, maybe she just happened to move out of the way when he was finished casting. Eiworth was never one to be considerate. Or maybe he was showing Fran courtesy for being a rare Black Sky Tiger.

Either way, Eiworth fired his spell when Fran moved out of the way.

"Blizzard! Giantsbane!"

Different elements—frost and deadly poison at the same time. Fran could only manage to cast two spells if they were of the same element. The old man was not to be trifled with.

Blizzard blew a miniature snowstorm around the target while forming blades made of ice to cut them. Giantsbane, as the name implied, produced a poison gas strong enough to kill giants. The two spells complemented each other perfectly. Blizzard covered the opponent with Giantsbane's poison gas, while the poison festered the skin enough for the ice to freeze them.

What's more, his spells weren't getting nullified.

Eiworth grinned when he caught her staring. Still, he looked a bit exhausted—probably because he cast two powerful spells at the same time. It was the first time the old man looked vulnerable.

"I saw how you beat those fanatics earlier with your grand spell. They can't completely nullify a spell past a certain point. In fact, the nullification perfectly tuned the area of effect for me."

Blizzard was supposed to have a wider area of effect, but the nullification shrank it to encapsulate the undead elephant. Eiworth had taken this into account when he overcharged the spells.

"I wasn't sure if it would work but it did! But I only would've hit the bugs if it didn't."

Dammit, Eiworth! You had my respect for a second there!

"Ooooorgh!"

Eiworth clicked his tongue. "These compound spells are enough to lock a dragon down. To think that it could still move after that..."

The mage used to be part of a party with Dragon Twist Dias, Dragon Hunter Phelms, and Dragon Hammer Gammod. He himself was known as Dragon Bind Eiworth.

The elephantman was stronger than he expected. He unleashed powerful winds from his body, dispelling both spells. Patches of his body were blackened by frostbite, but they soon healed themselves.

Eiworth chuckled. "Very interesting!"

He was in a tough spot, with his magic and potions rendered ineffective. Did he have other tricks up his sleeve? We kept watching him, in part so that we wouldn't get caught up in any of his attacks. In the end, Fran determined that magic wasn't going to be useful in this fight and tightened her grip around me.

We'll attack from above.

All right.

A falling attack from the sky. It was actually pretty good in her exhausted state, since she could leverage gravity to add to the attack. This aerial attack was also our specialty. I teleported us up into the sky. The insect rangers saw what Fran was trying to do and started redoubling their offense to keep the enemy's attention on the ground.

Fran's eyes met Robin's for a moment. The lobster leader looked stunning when he grinned. The bits of red shell covering his arms and face didn't detract from his looks. If anything, they only added to them!

Fran took a deep breath and started concentrating her energy. We wouldn't be able to take our opponent down in one hit. Fran couldn't Awaken now, let alone use Flashing Thunderclap. Meanwhile, my durability and mana were still shot from fighting Aschtner. We were in no condition to slash our enemy in two like we usually did.

Even so, we had to do this.

"We have to protect them all."

Yeah.

Garrus, the adventurers, everyone. Fran was ready to put her life on the line for them, and as her sword, I was ready too.

"Huh?"

It's the blue light.

The light connecting us started glowing again. Apparently, it wasn't restricted by our exhaustion or durability values. Our heightened resolve must have triggered it.

"Let's do this."

You got it!

Fran kicked the air with Air Hop and used a variety of skills to accelerate herself further, focusing all her energy on a single point for a piercing attack. She held me close to her side, pointing me straight down. Soon, she became too fast for the naked eye to see.

Enveloped by the blue light, Fran looked like a spear cast from heaven to destroy the undead elephant.

"Yaaaaah!"

"Raaaaagh!"

How did he see that?!

A barrier of wind protected the elephantman's head even as he fought the insect rangers. The winds whipped and whirled, stopping me in my tracks. An ordinary barrier wouldn't have stopped me—this thing was using his winds to grab me by the blade. I didn't think an undead was capable of such fine movements.

"Hngh...!"

Fran gritted her teeth and pushed but my cutting tip wouldn't go deeper.

But we had foreseen this. We figured that our initial attack probably wouldn't go well—it might even be blocked. I didn't want to do this, but...

Fran, are you ready?!

"Hm!"

Here goes!

I transformed myself into something without decoration or guard. I looked like a drill and started spinning myself like one using Mana Thruster. Fran had to hold on to stabilize me and her hands were beginning to bleed. Her own blood splattered as I advanced the attack. I didn't know how much her palms must hurt but I wasn't about to tell her to let go. We both knew that taking down this elephant would need extraordinary measures.

"Aaaaaaaaah!"

Yaaaaaargh!

I then exploded with the full force of Fanatix's mana thrusters and my own telekinesis. My mana thrusters swirled in a spiral and the explosion broke through the wind barrier. But the explosion also blew Fran away, and she flew in a tailspin toward the buildings. I was worried, but I couldn't stop now.

Haaaaaa!

Fran wouldn't get injured from that. If anything, I needed to finish our opponent here for her sake!

I plunged into the elephantman's right shoulder while still being wrapped in that blue light.

Dammit! He altered my trajectory!

I narrowly missed his head. The elephantman settled for changing my trajectory when he knew I was about to break through.

Fine, I can still do this! I'll just burn you from the inside!

I cast a Flame spell while inside him. You could have the toughest hide in the world, but no one would get off scot-free after being incinerated from the inside.

But my spell didn't go off—it was completely nullified. Apparently, even his insides were under the protection of the Fanatix replica.

I'll just have to find that replica!

I didn't know where it was, but I was sure I could find it if I kept digging with my blade.

"Nuooooh! Damn yooooou!"

I turned myself into a thin needle and started poking through the elephantman's body. He hardened his body with mana, making his flesh as hard as steel, but I took my time and prodded through the cracks with my tip. The undead elephant howled in pain and grabbed at me, trying desperately to pull me out. But I wasn't leaving that easily...

"Raaaaagh!"

...especially not when I had backup.

"All right guys, pile in on him!"

"Got it!"

The insect rangers took advantage of the distraction and started attacking. This time their attacks were less coordinated as each took to unleashing their hardest-hitting attacks on the elephant.

"Lead Fist!"

With his hips low to the ground, the lobster unleashed a straight attack. It must've been one of the Martial Arts Skills. What differentiated it from a regular punch was the hardened fist. It was several times more powerful than a regular martial artist's punch, and powerful enough to stagger the undead elephant when delivered to his right thigh.

"Ooooorgh!"

"Shadow Flash."

"Rargh?!"

Effie used another stealth attack—a Phantom spell which struck at the elephantman's weak point right as she came out of a shadow step. The tip of her spear was charged with mana, and it stabbed the creature's heart. It wasn't enough to kill the undead, but it would've been lethal against anyone else.

Meanwhile, Ann the bull ant's attack was ridiculously simple.

"Yah, yah, yah!"

She used her twin axes and chopped away to her heart's content. That's probably what she was going for, anyway. She used the opening Effie gave her to close in on the elephantman and hack away at his trunk. I think she struck him ten times over the span of a few seconds. Still, the elephantman spat blinding poison as his trunk flew away. He certainly wasn't going down without a fight.

Shingen the clam was up next.

"Hraaaagh!"

The big man, who occupied the strange slot of mage-tank, came at the enemy with his bare hands and started throwing them. The elephantman hadn't regenerated his legs and had no way of defending himself against the attack.

Shingen's strikes landed, but he wasn't doing much damage to the undead. But this was all part of the plan. He just needed to keep the enemy occupied so his teammates could get a clean hit in.

Hobbes finally made his move, and it was very clear-cut.

"Eat this! Blast Kick!"

First, he took some distance from the opponent and then broke into a dash. Using the momentum, he jumped to deliver a fast and powerful kick. It was simple, but the lack of complex motions meant the move preserved all of its force.

A grasshopper who delivers a flying kick...

Hobbes' rider kick broke through the wind barrier and hit the elephantman right in the chest.

"Gaaaah!"

The undead elephant staggered and fell, making a booming sound when his gigantic body landed on the ground. It was the first time in the fight that a physical hit had dealt significant damage.

"Cursed invaders! I will chase you out! *BAHROOOO!*"

The elephantman shouted hatefully as he used the winds to get back on his feet. The winds around him reacted to his voice, wrapping around him like a whirlwind, destroying anything that came near.

Melee was now out of the option. We would get torn to shreds if we tried.

"Violet Whirlwind!"

Violet Whirlwind?! That's the Class Skill of the Purple Wind Elephant!

"*FROOOOOMP!*"

The hurricane had a purple glow to it, and the smoke and light made it possible to see the flow of the usually invisible wind. Though the winds lost the advantage of being invisible, the deadly concentration of mana more than made up for it.

The elephantman lifted his arms to his sides, unleashing powerful gales of violet wind.

"Guaaah!"

"Kyaaaa!"

The wind pressure blew the insectoid halflings away—even they were helpless against it. The purple winds then formed spheres before flying out in all directions. Houses were immediately destroyed.

No! Stop that!

Fran wasn't back yet, so she was either unconscious or couldn't move. I didn't want to imagine what would happen if one of these winds managed to hit her.

"You will not defeat me!"

How are you so lively for an undead?!

"I am the shield of the kingdom! Guardian of the people! Protector of my allies!"

I respect your noble motivations, but I can't afford to lose this fight either!

I have to protect Fran!

"Gaaaaaah!"

I put all my effort into Transmogrify, extending my blade like roots into the soil. But the elephantman struggled, focusing his purple winds around my hilt. I thought the winds were going to attack me, but they were pulling me out instead. They almost succeeded too.

Hrngh!

"Guooooh!"

No wonder he's one of the Ten. I can't beat him in a test of strength!

My hilt hovered for a moment, and I was running out of mana to maintain my foothold.

But I can't lose now!

I wasn't at a complete disadvantage. The undead elephant's mana was draining away little by little. The Class Skill of the Ten Tribes took a lot of mana out of its user, be it Fran's Flashing Thunderclap, the Beast King's Golden Flame of Extinction, or this elephantman's Violet Whirlwind. He would've used it from the start if it didn't exhaust him. The longer he maintained the skill, the more mana he would expend.

And then backup finally came.

"Let's go!"

Robin and the rangers were back. They still hadn't lost their will to fight after being blasted by the powerful attack. They huddled up and got into a strange circular formation. Shingen was at the front, crouching as if he was about to sprint, while the other four readied themselves behind him. One by one, they used him as a launchpad to jump into the air. What's more impressive was that Shingen helped them take to the skies. The slightest misstep would've spelled failure.

Effie and Ann went first, and they whirled in the air.

Robin and Hobbes came next, and they planted their feet on top of the women's shins to kick themselves further above. They were now close to a hundred meters in the air, all without a Wind spell. It really drove home how strong and coordinated they were. But they weren't done just yet.

"Come on, Hobbes!"

"Try not to die, Robin!"

Robin pulled his knees to his chest and curled up into a ball. Hobbes pulled his leg back and kicked him like the protagonist of a soccer manga.

"GATE CRASHER!" they both shouted as Robin hurtled toward the ground like a meteor.

He shoots!

Robin was enveloped in the glow of mana, making him look even more like a soccer shot in a *manga*. Judging by the speed he was going, the attack would do tons of damage both to the enemy and to Robin himself. The attack's name suggested that it was a move reserved for breaking down a castle's gates.

"*BAHROOOO!*"

Purple winds blew in Robin's direction now, but they were helpless to stop his momentum. Still, the undead elephant was no mere undead. He immediately moved to avoid the attack once he knew he couldn't disarm it.

He blasted purple winds to where the attack was going to land and shifted away.

He's going to miss!

Or so I thought. But Robin wasn't done yet. There was a burst of mana, and the red ball of death suddenly changed course. Robin was chasing the elephant down with mana thrusters. He broke through the undead's wind barrier and rammed right into the side of his head. There was a loud crack as the creature's head exploded. There was nothing left of him from the neck up.

"Gaah...!"

Robin didn't come out of the attack unscathed. He had cracks all over his shell and his right hand was blown to bits. His bones were probably broken too. But in hindsight, he was fortunate that this was all he had to pay for an attack that powerful. His training and skill usage must've reduced the damage enough for him to survive.

I used a bit of my mana to help him. I couldn't heal him completely, of course, but it would be enough to prevent him from dying. I then realized how they were able to quickly understand what Fran was going for earlier. This attack was their trump card, and they knew what to do in case anyone else attempted something similar.

But we couldn't celebrate just yet.

Bone and muscle were already forming on the elephantman's neck to replace his destroyed head. Robin's desperate attempt to kill him had failed. The purple winds came at my hilt and they were as strong as before.

However, I could feel that particularly disgusting mana coming from his center now. There was a Fanatix replica buried inside him after all, and it was probably fused to his magicite. No wonder all that mana nullification didn't exhaust his mana. He had a backup mana source.

But now, the elephantman was finally out of mana, and he was forced to tap into the crystal and Fanatix replica. Robin couldn't kill him, but at least I now knew his weak spot. The replica was located somewhere in his core instead of in his back. I redoubled my efforts into transmogrifying myself, but the elephantman picked up on it. The violet winds picked up even while he was still bloodied and beaten.

Let go of me, you big lug!

"Raaaagh!"

I braced myself with mana, putting every ounce of power I had into staying inside him.

Aaargh...!

A dull, familiar pain ran through me. Was I falling apart again? Right after Aristea fixed me?

No... This pain is nothing if it means I can protect Fran! I have to keep going! I need more power!

—thing...

Yaaaaah!

Everything...

Huh? Who's there?

There was a voice, and it sounded like it was pretty close too. It probably wasn't the elephantman, though.

But there couldn't have been a voice because I wasn't sensing anyone in the vicinity. Was I hearing things after that intense pain?

Just a little more! I'm almost to his gut! That's where the replica is so please! Just give me a little more power!

I clenched my teeth and felt power flow through my body. I kept extending myself to find my target.

...cher!

Another hallucination?

Teacher!

Fran? You're okay!

Hm. I'm coming to get you!

It was Fran's voice, and I wasn't imagining it. Maybe Fran was the one talking to me too. I could've been concentrating so hard that I didn't hear her. I hadn't had to focus on telepathy in a while—we would usually just talk to each other in our heads.

"Haaaaa!"

Fran shouted as she charged the elephantman. She was completely defenseless and without a barrier.

Careful, Fran!

I'll be fine!

It sure didn't look that way to me! Unfortunately, as much as I wanted to protect her, I was in no position to do anything. If I teleported to her side, I would waste this once in a lifetime chance of taking down the elephantman.

The undead elephant saw Fran from the corner of his eye, breathed in, and pointed his trunk at her. A moment later, he fired an air cannon at her—with violet winds this time. This was much stronger than before.

If that thing hits her, she's—

"That won't work this time!"

Huh?

"Broomp?"

The elephant and I were both equally confused. A sheet of ice emerged in front of Fran, blocking the wind's advance. Eiworth was backing her up. No wonder she was so confident!

Fran had entrusted her life to Eiworth, the winner of Most Suspicious Person in the Capital Award. His strength definitely made him useful, but his attitude left much to be desired. But now wasn't the time to be choosy about allies.

God, Buddha, Eiworth! Please protect Fran!

I prayed earnestly, I didn't know whether they would be answered or not, but Fran managed to close in on the elephantman without a scratch. But now, the undead elephant unleashed a gust of wind which covered an impressive amount of ground in front of him.

"Teacher, your strap!" Fran reached out to me and shouted. I immediately extended my strap into her hand, still badly wounded from our earlier endeavor. She batted away the violet wind and brought her left hand to her mouth. There was something small and black inside it.

What is that?

Fran bit into it before I could Identify it. It must've been some kind of drug.

Suddenly, black lightning crackled all over Fran's body.

"Awaken! Flashing Thunderclap!"

What?! But I thought you were still exhausted!

"Haaaaa!"

"Raaaargh!"

Fran let the black lightning flow through me to burn the elephantman from the inside. The Fanatix replica reduced its power, but the direct current of black lightning was still powerful enough to stun an elephant. Or, in this case, an *undead* elephant.

Now's our chance...!

I had so many questions for her, but they would have to wait.

With the elephantman incapacitated, I resumed my search for the Fanatix replica and pierced through him. My cutting edge was now ripping through his body like butter.

You're done for!

I felt my blade cut something in half.

"RUAAAAAAAAAAAAAGH!"

The undead elephant let out a ghastly wail as the familiar sensation of mana absorption came over me.

We did it...

Even as an undead, a member of the Ten Tribes was still powerful.

Teacher, are you all right?

Yeah... Somehow.

Fran came over to the undead monster's corpse to pull me out of its flesh. She grunted as she tried to dislodge me, but getting me out was easy once I turned off Transmogrify. Once I was out, she rinsed me off with some water and scrubbed me down.

You turned black earlier.

Wait, what?

Hm. Your mana turned black and hazy before I called out to you.

Black and hazy...?

Never heard that one before. Was there something wrong with my mana? I was so focused on staying inside the enemy that I didn't know what was going on...

I'm worried. Are you sure you're okay?

Hang on, I'm the one who's worried about *you! What was that about?!*

Fran was no longer in her Awakened state, but she definitely used Flashing Thunderclap earlier. That shouldn't have been possible.

I'm fine. That was one of Eiworth's medicines.

That was what?! What were you thinking?!

Apparently, the drug temporarily restored you to peak vitality for a short period of time.

A-and there are no side effects?

I feel fine.

Are you sure?

Hm. I'll just get sleepy later and sleep for longer than usual.

You're not fine! How much longer are we talking?!

Uhhh, a lot?

Fran didn't know, either. If I had a mouth, I would've given Eiworth a piece of my mind. I wanted to ruffle Fran's hair so bad, but the old bastard in question came over.

"You won, somehow."

"Hm."

"That final blow," Eiworth said. "There aren't many people who can control their sword like that."

He scanned her up and down. It must've looked like Fran was controlling me when I killed the elephantman. Even Eiworth couldn't imagine a sword with a will of its own.

"And you're a C-Rank? How is that possible...? Has the guild gone senile?"

He recognized her unnatural strength. Fran was so strong for a C-Rank that it bordered on fraudulence.

"Ah, but maybe it's because you're young. Which guild do you belong to?"

"What?"

"What, are you a wanderer? Do you know Klimt or Amanda then? Or anyone in Alessa?"

I wasn't expecting to hear familiar names from this old man. I didn't think Eiworth and Amanda were acquainted with each other. I wouldn't have been surprised if they tried to start killing each other if they were ever in the same place.

"I know both of them," Fran said. "I became an adventurer in Alessa."

"That must be it," Eiworth nodded.

"What do you mean?"

"Amanda and Klimt are heavily opposed to sending children out onto the battlefield. And they are quite influential with the government of this country. Being under their wing would deter people from forcing promotions on you."

While the two of them probably did nothing to stop people from promoting Fran, the mere association was enough. A young adventurer who signed up in Alessa and was good friends with Amanda. No guildmaster was ignorant enough not to recognize her.

"The nobles get annoying once you hit B-Rank. They were the reason I quit."

Apparently, they were annoying enough to even ruffle Eiworth's feathers, and he was the very picture of insolence.

"That bad?"

"Indeed. You mustn't underestimate their network of information. They seek to recruit B-Ranks every chance they get. Some are modest, while others apply more direct pressure. But they all want the same thing: a strong adventurer working for them. They won't leave you alone until they have you."

"And if I refuse?"

"They'll act like they didn't get the message."

That sounded an awful lot like an old legendary mage. I guess Eiworth didn't like his own kind much. Still, he continued, ignorant of his shared faults.

"It's the same in any town in any kingdom in the world. There will always be nobility there," Eiworth said. "And when you make a name killing dragons like I did… Well, the invitations only get worse. Nobles will fight over you if they know how strong you are."

"I don't wanna have anything to do with them," Fran said.

"Doesn't matter. They're nobility, after all. In the end, you can't refuse them even if you try. If you do, they get offended and throw a tantrum." Eiworth scoffed, "What a load of nonsense."

For Eiworth, the daily dealings with nobles irritated him to the point of quitting the Adventurer's Guild. He could've become a guildmaster like Gammod and Dias, but he refused.

"I wouldn't have time for my research then."

These weren't the only options, of course. Amanda and Forlund dealt with nobles every now and again and even worked for them to protect them from other nobility. But Eiworth wasn't the type to make that kind of relationship work, and Fran fell in the same category. She might cause problems by punching her employers in the face. Maybe she would learn to deal with it better when she was older, but for now, I wanted things to remain as they were.

What surprised me was Klimt's alleged clout. He was strong, but he didn't feel that strong for an A-Rank... Maybe he had accumulated respect for his long years of serving as guildmaster.

Fran asked Eiworth about Klimt and he smirked.

"You can't judge a sorcerer by his stats alone. A powerful sorcerer can control hordes of invisible beasts, you know."

I didn't quite understand what sorcery was. I'd seen the spirits that Klimt and others like him used, but they didn't seem that strong or stealthy to me. Eiworth explained that the spirits sorcerers used could be hard to detect, granting them protean strategies. Now Klimt was one of the greatest sorcerers in the continent, let alone the kingdom.

"Do you know what people call him? Calamity Klimt."

"Calamity?"

That sounds violent.

"He's a walking calamity that brings down destruction on friend and foe alike." Eiworth shrugged, "It's not true, of course, but that's his nickname."

"What's more, his abilities far surpass the average A-Rank. Ah, but I suppose he's retired now so he would be a former A-Rank... Either way, he could give S-Ranks a run for their money in battle."

The guildmaster was that powerful? There might've been more to this Spirit Magic than I once thought.

Now that I thought about it, Alessa was surrounded by dangerous environments. The Demon Wolf's Garden, an A-Rank haunt. Dungeons. Raydoss. You had to be strong to be the guildmaster of that town.

"But enough talk about old Calamity. You are far more interesting than he is."

Eiworth looked intently at Fran.

"All that power at such a young age. Very interesting indeed. What say you let me perform an autopsy on you? One million gauld, and I'll guarantee your safety."

"No."

"Two million! Come on, now. It will only take a little while. I just want a peek at your magic circuits!"

"Not happening."

"I-I suppose I can't persuade you?"

"Hm."

Erianthe came to our side as the ridiculous conversation carried on.

"We'll be fine for now, Fran," she said. "Can I trouble you to head to the palace?"

"The palace?"

"Yes. I can't get a hold of the knights there, but I'm sure they need help evacuating people."

There was a huge surge of mana coming from the direction of the palace. Things were probably worse there than anywhere else in the capital.

"Okay."

Fran wouldn't be able to fight, but she could still look for survivors. I really wanted her to rest, but she was as driven as ever. The adrenaline probably made her forget about her exhaustion.

"I'm coming with you!"

"No. You're staying at the guild to help the mages."

Erianthe stopped Eiworth before he could get another word in.

"We don't have enough of them, and I would like you to teach our mages how to deal with the fanatic soldiers."

"Then get the court mages if you're lacking manpower!" Eiworth said, and then paused. "Wait, is it that time of the year again?"

"Yes. Aschtner must've planned around it."

"What are you guys talking about?"

"The haunt hunt."

The reason why the ranks of knights and mages were only at half strength was because they were being sent to deal with the nearby haunt. The haunt itself was only a C-Rank, so it wasn't inherently dangerous. However, once every four years, there would be an outbreak of locust monsters and the king's men would be sent there to deal with them. Marquis Aschtner knew about this, and so he planned to launch his coup at this season.

"As a reward, I'll remove the bounties from your head."

"Bounty?" Fran asked.

"You've seen how he behaves. It's only natural that he would gather up some bounties over the years."

"I see."

Fran and I nodded at the same time. It would've been strange if Eiworth *didn't* have a bounty of some sort.

"I can even give you an actual reward from the guild."

Eiworth scoffed, "I've never even noticed I had a price on my head. You can keep it on there. But if you insist on rewarding me… How about you give me the samples you've captured after all this is over?"

Erianthe was silent for a while. Eventually, she said, "I'll try to acquire some for you."

"Excellent. Very well, I'll make good use of your mages."

"Don't go too crazy out there."

"I know."

"Doesn't seem that way to me," Erianthe sighed. She had to gather whatever support she could for the guild.

She didn't want Eiworth's help, but she couldn't deny the old man's strength on the battlefield. She had to make it worth his while.

"We really are counting on you."

Eiworth chuckled, "Yes, yes, I know."

He definitely didn't.

I guess that's the last we'll see of Eiworth for a while. Can't say I'm going to miss him.

Hm. We need to check in on Garrus.

Yeah. We have to get the guild to take care of him.

Fran entered the guild building. It looked like a field hospital now, with how many injured people were inside. Stellia was the first to notice her.

"Thanks again, Fran! We couldn't have made it without you. Garrus is inside."

"Hm. Thanks."

"No, no, the pleasure's all ours!"

Stellia called one of her subordinates to take Fran to him. Garrus was still unconscious, but there wasn't a scratch on him.

"I want you to take care of Garrus," Fran said. She explained that he was unconscious because of the drugs they gave him and that he would need further treatment to improve. The enemy might also try to take him back.

Stellia knitted her eyebrows. She wasn't sure the guild could take care of the blacksmith with all the other injured people lying around.

"Just accept her request. Is there any reason to think about it?"

Eiworth suddenly joined the conversation. Apparently, Fran was now the subject of his curiosity. Not good.

Stellia glared at the rude old man. Stellia-versus-Eiworth was going to be the match of the century.

"And who the hell are you?" Stellia started. Her voice made it clear that she didn't trust this newcomer. To be honest, I hoped they wouldn't come to blows in the middle of all these people...

"I am Eiworth. I used to be an adventurer."

But Stellia's attitude soon did a one-eighty. Her frown was replaced by a look of admiration. The look of a girl in love. The old lady still had it in her.

"S-Sir Eiworth? You mean you're Dragonbind Eiworth?"

Her voice was at a higher pitch now. Sweeter too. Eiworth paid it no mind and took something out of his pocket.

"Yes. Here's my old guild card."

"S-scanning now!"

Stellia accepted Eiworth's guild card with trembling hands. She scanned it to confirm its authenticity.

"I-it's real! You really *are* Sir Eiworth! I knew you were in the capital, but I never thought I'd get to meet you in person!" Stellia squealed. She stared at the card for a few moments in disbelief before returning it to him. "I-I'm honored!"

"Indeed."

Stellia went from a lady of iron to an fangirl over the course of a few seconds. There were stars in her eyes as she stared at her longtime idol. Her voice was still a pitch higher compared to before. The other receptionists stared at her, shocked at the change in personality.

"So, can you take care of the dwarf?" Eiworth asked.

"Y-yes! Yes, of course!"

Eiworth's less-than-polite tone didn't bother Stellia in the slightest. She must've really looked up to him. I still wasn't sure whether the guild would be up to it though.

"Are you sure?" Fran asked. "The enemy might come for him."

"We'll be fine. You can count on it. I used to be a B-Rank in my heyday myself, you know! I'll start calling the high ranks who aren't here immediately! And some alchemists and mages to treat Garrus, as well!"

Is she going to ask the high ranks for help again?

Stellia chuckled and continued. "How many years do you think I've been a receptionist? I know enough about adventurers to pull some strings. I'd never loan them out to some random noble, but for you, Sir Eiworth, anything!"

Apparently, Stellia was the secret boss of the capital's guild. She should be able to handle this.

Leaving Garrus under the guild's care was probably the best option. I got nervous thinking about what would happen if we handed him over to the government. Like it or not, the blacksmith *was* implicated in the production of Godsword replicas, perhaps even the restoration of a broken Godsword. People in power could just enslave him to have him go on producing more replicas.

The Adventurer's Guild was a safer place for him, in that sense. Fran returned to the counter to add one last bit of insurance. A bag of coins hit the counter with a thud. One million gauld in all. Stellia looked surprised at the gesture.

"I'm issuing a quest. Get Garrus back on his feet and keep him safe. Don't hand him over to anyone other than me—especially not the government." Fran pointed to the money bag, "This will cover the reward and expenses."

"I'll sign my name on the quest too," Eiworth said. "Don't want the government blindsiding us."

"I'll make sure your quest is fulfilled, Sir Eiworth! Shouldn't be too hard to find takers, considering the hefty reward."

Now it was an official Adventurer's Guild quest. If anything happened to Garrus, the guild would have to answer for it.

"So what's the situation?" Fran asked.

"Oh, right," Stellia said. "Well, you see—"

As expected, the noble district was a warzone. However, Fran was not listening to Stellia's explanation in the slightest. She was duking it out in her own battle with sleep. She nodded awake once, but that was all she could do. Eventually, she drifted off to sleep as Stellia was still talking.

"Black Lightning? You listening?" the receptionist asked. All she got from Fran was the rhythmic breathing of sleep.

Whoa!

She almost fell back in her seat, but Stellia grabbed hold of it in the nick of time. There was a loud thud as the chair's feet hit the ground.

"Oh, dear. I suppose there's no helping it."

Stellia wasn't mad, not at all. On the contrary, she picked Fran up with a gentle smile on her face. She was like a grandmother tucking her granddaughter to sleep. She really was a good person.

"She looks like every other kid when she's asleep," Eiworth chuckled.

Meanwhile, this old man is still looking at her like she's a test subject!

"Wh-what shall we do?"

I don't think you should ask Eiworth about what to do here. Whatever he says, don't do it!

"Hmph. Let the runt rest. She's not much good on the field the way she is."

"All right."

Huh.

I wasn't expecting that at all. I thought for sure he was going to ask Stellia to lay Fran down on the table so he could dissect her. Then again, I guess Eiworth was one to play by the rules. I was worried that I was going to have to protect Fran from him, so that was one bullet dodged. I was ready to reveal my true identity if it came to it.

"I'll be off then. She is a valuable subject whom I wish to observe. Don't kill her."

"U-understood! Good luck out there!"

"Indeed."

It felt like there was a budding romance between the middle-aged woman and the old man...except Eiworth was completely uninterested in her. Whatever unreciprocated crush was going on, it made me uncomfortable.

Soon, the room was empty. The able-bodied had headed back to the field while the ones taking care of the injured were making their rounds.

Fran continued to sleep.

I need to get to the root of the situation if I want to keep Fran safe.

Fanatix, the Godsword, had been controlling Marquis Aschtner. Someone had to deal with the lunatic Godsword, but as much as I wanted to stop it, I couldn't leave Fran by herself. Its fanatics could attack her at any moment. She was probably a high-priority target now, considering how she defeated the marquis.

What to do...

Conflicting voices raged within my mind.

That Godsword must not be allowed to exist!

You must destroy it!

Wipe out its very existence from the world!

For some reason, part of me hated Fanatix so much that I was beginning to hear things. Was it because I was also a discarded Godsword? Maybe this was the source of my revulsion for the replicas.

I felt like these voices had gotten louder after we defeated the undead elephantman. But even so, my mind was made up.

I have to protect Fran!

The revulsion within me was so strong that it was beginning to torment my mind. I was worried that I might go crazy. Once I started being aware of the hatred in my heart, its strength multiplied.

Even so, I couldn't leave. I was Fran's sword. Her safety was my top priority.

I can't just leave her, but...

Suddenly, the mana in the room shifted. Mana was gathering in a dark corner of the room where the sun didn't shine. Teleportation. I watched and kept my guard up.

"Urf..."

Jet came through the portal. I remained calm, but...

Y-you're hurt!

"Woof..."

There were deep wounds all over his body, and he looked like he'd lost a lot of blood. I started healing him.

What happened to Frederick and Velmeria?

"Ruff...!"

Jet barked pitifully. They had failed to save her, it seemed. He used Brain Trick, a Shadow spell which allowed him to reveal his memories to someone else.

No... Velmeria...!

"Woof."

And Frederick stayed behind to buy you time.

Fanatix was controlling Velmeria now, and it was far more powerful than before. She was wielding a broken sword, probably the genuine Fanatix, so the level of possession she was experiencing must've been a cut above the rest.

"Woof!"

Jet took out a piece of metal the size of a hand from the shadows.

And you found this while you were there...

It was the tip of a sword. The mana coming from it was strange. It wasn't particularly strong, but it felt familiar somehow. I felt drawn to it, and just looking at it calmed me down. This metal shard had the opposite energy of the feelings which emerged when I thought of Fanatix and its replicas.

What is this... No way!

"A-arf?"

Sorry for shouting, boy. Apparently, this thing is the tip of Holy Order.

"Woof?"

Yeah, seriously.

The Holy Spirit Sword known as Holy Order. It was said to have been destroyed when it fought Fanatix to a draw. Though not much was known of its powers, it was created by the first Godsmith specifically to combat Fanatix.

What was a piece of it doing here? Fanatix was apparently excavated out of some ruins, so maybe this shard was excavated along with it.

What are Holy Order's powers anyway...?

I Identified it but its name was only listed as Holy Order Shard. If we could utilize its powers, we might have a shot at beating Fanatix.

Hang on. That's not out of the question.

Cannibalize. What if I could use it on the Holy Order Shard? Would I gain some of its powers? Even an ounce of it would come in handy right now. If nothing else, I would be able to recover some of my own strength. It was worth a shot.

Can I have this shard, Jet?

"Woof!"

All right, here goes!

I lifted the shard and cut it in two, and a tremendous surge of power immediately rushed through me.

Aaaaaargh!

"Bark! Woof!"

I'm...fine...!

I didn't feel like throwing up, unlike Fanatix. I was just overwhelmed by the sheer amount of power the small shard gave me. It was the power of a real Godsword. A weapon far stronger than I could hope to be.

It gave me a lot of my mana back!

The shard recovered most of the mana I spent fighting Aschtner and the elephantman, but it didn't give me any new skills or increase my powers.

Unfortunate, but having more mana is always a good thing. I'm feeling strangely good too.

I might be able to take on Fanatix now. The fight wouldn't be completely one-sided, at least.

I scanned the city for the Godsword and picked up several mana signatures of interest. Apparently, I could sense the Fanatix replicas' mana better than before. It was probably because I had just absorbed Holy Order's power. I focused on the one I suspected of being Fanatix itself and found that it was located near the palace. This one's mana signature was the biggest too.

I think this is the one.

Someone came into the room then, probably Stellia. Her footsteps were rushed and erratic.

Did something happen?

"Who's there?!" she said, and then sighed. "Oh, it's just Black Lightning's familiar. You had me scared there for a second."

Jet whined apologetically. I guess it was only normal

for her to freak out after suddenly sensing a monster in the building.

"I'm glad you're here though. We're about to evacuate the injured and non-combatants to outside the city. I'm sure I can leave the princess in your paws."

"Arf!"

"There's a good boy."

"Woof?"

"What's that? You want to know what's going on? Aah, if only our meathead adventurers were half as smart as you are! Here's the deal."

Stellia gave Jet a rundown of the situation. A drake girl was rampaging near the castle, decimating the knights trying to stop her. She was so powerful that nothing they could do could stop her. Forlund was present at the site, but he had been gravely wounded in the battle against the drake.

Hundred Blade Forlund, an A-Rank adventurer. He could summon and control countless swords at will. Every time I saw him fight, it reminded me of how he was at the top of my "People I Don't Want to Fight" chart. Frankly, he was so much stronger than we were that we couldn't possibly beat him. And yet Forlund couldn't last five minutes against Fanatix.

But that wasn't all.

An S-Rank adventurer had suddenly appeared and began fighting the drake.

S-Rank? Are there S-Ranks here?

Jillbird was home to Dimitris, Colbert's former master and an S-Rank adventurer. He was a genius martial artist and founder of the Dimitris Combat Arts. The only thing was that he wasn't in the capital at the moment.

"You ever heard of a man called Friendly Fire?"

Friendly Fire? You mean Urslars *is here?!*

"Arf? Woof, woof!"

So a young drake who easily took out an A-Rank... That had to be Velmeria, being controlled by Fanatix. The fact that she was fighting Urslars didn't bode well for the city. The destruction of nearby property was a given, but Urslars had a certain condition which caused him to lose control of himself if he fought for too long. The guild was well aware of it.

"You know him too? Then I don't need to tell you how terrifying he is. *He* might end up destroying the capital."

Because of that, the guild decided to evacuate the wounded. Would that work? He was restricted by the confined space of a dungeon last time, but this time we wouldn't be so lucky. A berserk Urslars could certainly level the capital, and its surroundings wouldn't be spared either. Could they even make it out of the capital while carrying the injured?

The best-case scenario would be if everyone were evacuated and Urslars defeated Velmeria without losing control or taking her life. The worst that could happen would be him losing control mid-fight. There would be a huge amount of collateral damage with how strong those two were. Even Fran and Garrus might be in danger.

So what now? The easiest course of action for me would be to put Fran on top of Jet and leave the capital behind, but Fran wouldn't like that when she woke up. Even worse, she might get upset and retaliate. Even if I managed to convince her to escape, she wouldn't be able to forgive herself for abandoning Erianthe and the others.

Which means we somehow have to beat Velmeria as quickly as possible to minimize the chance of Urslars going berserk.

I didn't even know if I could handle Fanatix on my own. Confronting two monsters at the same time was going to be tough. I was basically at half strength, and about the only thing I had going for me was the element of surprise.

Stealth was going to be critical here. I wouldn't be able to take Velmeria head-on. I could sneak into the battlefield, deal significant damage to Velmeria, and then support Urslars for the rest of the fight.

The palace plaza...

I could feel the tremendous mana signature.

Jet, I'm going to take care of Fanatix. You take care of Fran for me.

"Arf!"

If things go really bad, you take Fran and run. Got it?

"Woof!"

Jet barked and nodded. I wouldn't have to worry about them. He really was a reliable familiar.

I'll be off then.

Fran continued her peaceful sleep, and I intended to keep it that way.

Reincarnated as a sword

4

Clash of the Titans

I FELT THE SHIFT in the air as I flew toward the palace. The unsettling mana around the capital was mostly gone now. At this point, the fanatics had either self-destructed or dried up from Unleashed Potential.

The only mana signature left was Velmeria's, and it chilled me to the bone. I wanted to get closer to make sure it was really her, but I couldn't. The palace plaza was now a hellscape. It used to be a beautiful place, full of stone statues and carvings, but now the only stone features left were craters carved into the earth. Other parts of the plaza were perfectly flat, and I remembered seeing them in the Beastman Nation. They must have been Urslars' creation.

The surrounding mansions were destroyed, and the palace's walls were crumbling. I could no longer tell where the plaza started. There was a large hole in the barrier around the palace. Its beautiful spires had fallen, and its white walls were now burnt black.

And still, the hellscaping continued.

SHOOM!

KABOOM!

Two sets of monstrous mana slammed into each other, repulsing anyone that came near. Anyone too close to the scene would probably just disintegrate.

"Raaaaaagh!" Urslars shouted, swinging Gaia in its unleashed state.

I thought he was going to flatten the area with gravity, but instead, he flung a giant boulder at Velmeria. The boulder crashed into a shock wave of her mana, breaking into pieces and carving more destruction. I watched as a random noble's mansion was squashed beneath its weight.

Was I too late? Had Urslars already lost control? No, he was still lucid. The bloodred aura of Mad Ogre Form hadn't enveloped him yet. Still, if he was fighting this hard and causing so much destruction, then his opponent must have been powerful.

Meanwhile, Velmeria didn't seem like the woman I remembered at all. She teleported across the battlefield so quickly that I could only get a visual on her when she stopped.

She looked completely different. Although her blue hair remained the same, the rest of her body was now covered with scales the same color as her hair. Her arms, and other parts of her body, were enlarged, making her appear inhuman. As if that wasn't enough, there were gigantic wings on her back too. They looked a lot like dragon wings, and if they worked the same way, they probably used mana to accelerate her through the sky. A reptilian eye peeked out from her disheveled hair, and yet, I didn't sense any hostility from Velmeria herself—possibly because she was under Fanatix's control. Still, her lack of emotion only made her even *more* lizard-like.

While Urslars fought mainly with Land Magic, Velmeria used a variety of attacks. She zoomed across the battlefield blasting spells at the big man. I couldn't figure out why she hadn't taken to the skies, but both of them moved across the field so fast that they were invisible to the naked eye. Still, their powerful clashes were visible enough. Each attack was strong enough to destroy me. Their stray bullets blew holes in the ground, and their shock waves sent rubble flying. I could only watch from a distance, helpless to even approach.

"Burn to ashes!"

Velmeria created a miniature sun which descended slowly to the ground. It burned the air around it and boiled the earth. I could feel the heat of it, even from this distance. The stone pillar next to me started to bubble and melt. My durability began to drop, so I flew away before I turned into a puddle too.

The amount of mana in that spell made my fully charged Kanna Kamuy look like nothing. It was probably a grand Flame spell and, considering how powerful Velmeria was, I guessed it was Level 8 or 9. Either way, there's no way I could pull that off. Even Urslars hadn't managed to avoid the attack.

"Gaaaaaargh!"

Surprisingly, he jumped away from the miniature sun. His body was smoking, and his arms and face were covered in burns, but somehow, he survived—although I couldn't imagine how.

Urslars manipulated gravity to escape, then turned back to the miniature sun. He swiped at it with Gaia, shrinking it, and then eliminating it completely. The powerful gravity must've caused the sun to implode. The only thing left was a perfectly smooth dent in the earth, perhaps fifty meters in diameter, where the ground had just evaporated. Somehow, Urslars had managed to erase the powerful spell with one swing, and now it was his turn to attack. He created a small black sphere where the miniature sun used to be. This ball was only about thirty centimeters wide, but its effects were immediate. Bits of rubble and earth all flew toward the sphere. It must've been emitting a powerful gravitational field.

Oh, crap!

It was so strong! And I was starting to get sucked into it. I teleported again and again to get away. The area of effect was even wider than Velmeria's miniature sun. The sphere sucked in everything around it—parts of the palace wall, bits of ground, everything. The rubble crashed into each other, creating an expanding stone tornado while the plaza rumbled beneath their feet. I wouldn't be surprised if the entire capital felt it.

And Velmeria...? There she is!

She was on all fours, clinging to a gigantic rock as it whirled in the air. But rubble soon crashed into her rock island, throwing her away. She was overtaken by what looked like a small mountain and was pulled into the eye of the storm. The pressure from the gravity must've been insane.

KABOOM!

I thought Urslars had it in the bag when the explosion happened. A small mountain exploded from inside the black sphere, scattering boulders all over the place. Most of them fell inside the noble district, but even the smaller rocks tore right through roofs and walls. If you were to get hit by one, you would be gravely wounded. They rained destruction down on the already destroyed district, while Velmeria retaliated with a Water spell—creating a gigantic eight headed water snake to attack Urslars. The heads alone were close to ten meters long, and its sheer size was enough to make it deadly. But it was destroyed by a single swing of Gaia, and droplets of water fell to the ground like a downpour. However, the snake was only there to restrict Urslars' movements while Velmeria prepared her *real* attack. It was a very familiar attack too.

Kanna Kamuy...!

Velmeria's Kanna Kamuy was nothing like mine, and I felt utter defeat as I watched her cast it. I hadn't felt this way since Murelia, but at least back it felt like there was a chance I could catch up to her. The sense of defeat I felt this time was closer to despair. The difference in our power was too great. There was no contest.

Unlike Murelia's restricted Kanna Kamuy, Velmeria focused on power alone. Her bolt of lightning was thicker than anything I had ever seen. The thunderbolt pierced the ground and exploded. I could feel the shock waves, even from where I was floating. This was a *real* grand spell. A spell that could decimate armies with a single cast. It exceeded human limits. *That* was the true power of Kanna Kamuy.

My existence in this world didn't make sense, but this fight made even less. A single hit from one of them should've been enough to kill the other, but Urslars and Velmeria kept fighting. Their regenerative capabilities outpaced their attacks, so overtaking each other in one hit was difficult. Still, I couldn't just stand here and wait for the fight to end. Even in the chaos of combat, I saw something that forced me to act.

Urslars' horn is getting redder...

That was the first symptom of Mad Ogre Form. If you saw it once, you wouldn't forget it for the rest of your life.

If this keeps up, he might go berserk before the battle is over.

The hellscape, which so far had been limited to the palace plaza, might end up spreading to the rest of the city. These two monsters could destroy whole areas with a single attack. Without restrictions, they could even destroy the whole capital.

I have to end this fight before Urslars goes berserk.

Although most of the citizens had probably evacuated already, I couldn't let him lose control. The threat of him spreading this destruction to the outskirts of town was all too real. After watching these two titans go at it, I couldn't count on Urslars winning the day.

I should help him, but how...?

Both of them had too much life, and too high defense for my attacks to make any difference. The best I could do was create an opening for Urslars, but even then, I couldn't be sure that he would beat her. And besides, how was I supposed to make an opening for him in the first place?

I'll have to aim for Fanatix.

The mana coming out of Velmeria's broken sword rivaled Gaia's, so it had to be the real Fanatix. I only had to take one look at it to know it was a Godsword. No Identify required. I was strangely confident about that. Maybe it was the voice of P.A. whispering to me in my mind. Maybe it was because I'd just absorbed part of Holy Order. Either way, that broken sword was the root of all this chaos.

I need to do something about it...

That's when I noticed something. Fanatix was getting shorter. It wasn't as long as it was back when I arrived at the scene of this battle. Upon closer inspection, I saw that its blade was actually *disintegrating*. Godsword Unleash must be too strong for it. Its blade couldn't handle all that power.

Am I even needed here? It's only a matter of time until it self-destructs.

But Urslars might lose control before that happened, and I couldn't afford to take that chance.

It's a risk, but one I'll have to take.

If I hadn't seen the unleashed Gaia in action before, I would've been scared stiff. Seeing two Godswords duking it out would traumatize just about anyone.

But even so...

What to do?

I can't just go in there without a plan.

There was no way I could deal enough damage to Fanatix to destroy it in one hit. The best I could hope for was to land the perfect attack at the perfect time. Unleash Potential was out of the question—I couldn't handle it the way I was. Besides, I wanted to beat Fanatix *and* return to Fran in one piece.

Teleport into Telekinetic Catapult?

No. Fanatix was strong enough to sense me before I got close. And besides, the A-Ranks I'd fought with Fran had managed to dodge it, and Velmeria was far beyond an A-Rank at this point.

Without Fran around, I was at a huge disadvantage. Usually, I would just teleport us to a favorable location so Fran could land the killing blow. Coordinating our attacks like that kept our openings to a minimum. But alone? I was far less powerful.

What if I grabbed it with telekinesis?

If I could hold Fanatix for even a second, then I could land a hit. And if I used telekinetic guides like a railway, that would decrease the chances of me missing. On the flip side, using all my strength on telekinesis would lower my own attack power. Telekinetic Catapult wouldn't be the boss buster it usually was. But if I didn't hold onto the Godsword with all I had, it would break free.

What if I used magic—huh?

Suddenly, I felt someone approaching me. They were cloaked with Stealth Skills, but their invisibility faltered slightly when they dodged a giant block of rubble. They slipped into cover behind some rubble about twenty meters away from me.

I used Eagle Eye and other Observational Skills to see who it was. Their Stealth Skills were good, but you could see through them if you knew where to look. It was a man, crouching behind the ruins, his black hair tied in a knot. He was quite handsome and donned black armor.

He's alive! I knew he wouldn't die so easily!

It was Forlund. He probably wanted to know how the fight was going, despite the inherent danger of spectating. Still, something struck me as odd. Forlund didn't have Stealth Skills the last time I Identified him, but now he blended into the shadows perfectly, like an elite scout. I Identified him again, and soon found the reason for the change: the sword in his right hand. Forlund was taking advantage of his Extra Skill, Beloved of the Sword God.

CLASH OF THE TITANS

It allowed him to produce magic swords and take full advantage of their skills. The sword in his right hand had Stealth Skills, and the sword in his left was the same.

Now that I thought about it, that was a *very* powerful ability. The skill allowed him to produce any sword to fit the situation. And he could produce over a hundred at a time. That was like having over a hundred skills! Fran and I achieved a similar effect through Skill Sharing, but still, it was nothing to scoff at.

Should I cooperate with him? If I did, I'd have to talk to him as a sword—Doppelganger was still on cooldown.

Forlund...

Still, the man was definitely trustworthy, and I didn't mind revealing my identity to him. I'd seen nothing but good things from him so far. I mean, he was terrifyingly strong on the battlefield, but he was never hostile toward Fran. Maybe I was stereotyping here, but the strong and silent swordsman didn't seem the type to spread secrets. Maybe that was why I took a liking to him. Fran had never actually talked to him, but she seemed fond of him too. Besides, this was an emergency, and I had no time to hesitate. If cooperating with Forlund increased our chances of survival, I should do it. With my mind made up, I sent him a message.

Forlund, can you hear me?

Hm? What is this voice? Who are you?

Uhh, I'm not an enemy. I'm the Black Lightning Princess' teacher. I'm talking to you telepathically.

Are you? Very well. You don't seem hostile, at least.

And just like that, he believed me. Still, I wasn't going to complain. It wasn't like we had time for a cross-examination.

There's something I want to ask you.

What is it?

Do you have a way of defeating Velmeria—the drake girl? Any trump cards?

If Forlund already had a plan, then all I had to do was support him.

No. I don't have enough firepower. Her powers are far beyond the realm of human comprehension.

I see.

I fought with her earlier and was forced to flee.

How are your wounds?

I almost died, but I'll manage. How about you? Any ideas?

Some... By the way, that skill of yours, the one where you shoot out swords. Does it only work with your own equipment?

No. I do use it to control the swords I produce, but it allows me to control any sword within its range.

Telepathy, but only for swords. That might just work. It meant I could focus on holding down the enemy with Telekinesis, while Forlund launched his swords.

I was surprised by how talkative Forlund was. He'd always been a man of few words when we saw him, but inside his head, he talked as much as any other person. Maybe he just wasn't very good at putting his thoughts into speech. Either way, I felt like I knew him a little better now.

I need your powers, Forlund. Will you help me?
All right. What do you need?

He didn't even hesitate. What a reliable guy. I just hoped he wouldn't be taken aback at my existence.

Let's meet up. I'll head to your position. Just don't be too shocked when you see me.

I felt his confusion. I cut off comms and flew over.

"Hunh?"

Stay calm. I'm Teacher, an Intelligent Weapon.

"I see…"

Uhh…

"Very well."

That's it?

Forlund was convinced right away. I felt embarrassed for my smug little "Stay calm"! Couldn't he have acted at least a *little* bit surprised?!

D-do you know of other Intelligent Weapons?

"No."

Oh. I see...

Out loud, he was even less chatty than I remembered.

We can talk in your mind as long as we're connected. Would you prefer that?

Sure, if you want.

Everyone must tell you you're pretty quiet.

Not everyone. Some do.

I guess most people were too afraid to point it out. Either way, he was willing to cooperate, and so I told him my plan. It was all very simple: a high-speed surprise attack that used Forlund's powers, my skills and spells, and Dimension Gate to accelerate me further. The target was Fanatix, the sword in Velmeria's hands. In the best-case scenario, we would destroy it. More realistically, I hoped to weaken it with Cannibalize.

I had to kill something for the skill to activate, but that rule didn't seem to apply to Fanatix. I guess destroying part of it would count. Fanatix contained all the minds it had absorbed. Its thoughts, words, and memories were all amalgamations of the people it attacked. That much I knew for sure. So my attack would hurt part of it, even *kill* part of it. That was enough for Cannibalize to activate. That's exactly what happened with the replicas, so I knew it would work. Hopefully, Cannibalizing its abilities would weaken it enough for Urslars to destroy it. If things went well, it would at least speed up Fanatix's self-destruction.

The only issue was whether or not I could handle it. Sure, I could take the pressure of Forlund's Skill, but I was worried about what would happen to my mind when Cannibalize triggered. I also wanted to tell Urslars about the plan, but he was out of telepathy range. If I got any closer, Velmeria might detect me by then.

The other question is if we can deal enough damage.

In the end, we were up against a Godsword. Something that could survive even Urslars' attacks.

I can't Cannibalize it if we don't hurt it enough.

I told Forlund the rough idea of the plan. It was kind of pathetic after all my talk about having a plan, but even the best of them needed polishing. I thought he might bail on me. Instead, Forlund immediately gave a suggestion. He was such a good guy. Not that I'd hand Fran over to him!

How about this then? he said.

But if we do that—

However—

Look—

We bounced ideas off each other until the plan was formed.

This could work, Forlund said.

You're sure about that?

Yes. My life is a small price to pay to defeat that thing.

I'd rather you didn't die, but don't hold back either, okay?

Of course. You don't have to worry about me.

This plan would take a huge toll on Forlund, but it was much better than what I came up with myself. That said, the chances of success were still low.

We'll put a stop to this battle, said Forlund.

Yeah! Although, I should warn you about something. If anyone other than Fran equips me, they'll die. I'm serious. Just holding me is okay, though.

Really? Very well then. I'll be careful.

Uhh, are you sure?

About what?

Aren't you scared of holding me?

Of course. I won't equip you though, so there won't be a problem. The A-Rank had nerves of steel. *I should also warn you though.*

Huh? About what?

About my skill, Beloved of the Sword God. It analyzes enchanted swords, so it can make copies of them. I don't think it can reproduce you, but it should be able to analyze you—which means I might end up knowing all your secrets. And it activates automatically, so I can't do anything about it.

I see.

Still, I was prepared for that eventuality. Even with this inconvenience, refusing his help was not an option. We needed every edge we could get.

Well, I said. *If you do see anything, just don't tell anyone.*

"Of course."

Even without Essence of Falsehood, I believed him. Such was the advantage of the good and honest man. I didn't even really mind telling him my secrets.

We'll attack when Urslars pins Velmeria down, I said.

Yes. We'll put everything into that attack.

I'm counting on you.

Likewise, he said. *If anything, you play the bigger role here. You have to stop that girl.*

You got it. I'll give it everything I got.

"Good."

Forlund then produced ten swords, beginning with one named Sword of Trueshot Ambush—an enchanted sword which increased his accuracy. Next, he made swords of telekinesis and swords with the ability to manipulate the wind. Thanks to Beloved of the Sword God, he didn't need to hold all these weapons to gain their benefits. Finally, he produced an enchanted sword which was a cut above the rest. The blade was short, but its presence was anything but. If anything, the swordbreaker had a terrible aura around it. The back of its blade looked like it was made out of an animal's fang. If I didn't know that I was a discarded Godsword, then it could've been my rival. It was that threatening.

That your trump card?

Yes. The Demon Wolf's Jaw. The blade was made from the fang of Fenrir, the great devourer.

Fenrir...

I felt a strange familiarity when I heard that name and couldn't help but take an interest. Was Fenrir really sealed away inside me? It was only a theory, but perhaps the great wolf did have something to do with me after all.

What is it? Forlund asked.

Oh. Uhh, it's nothing.

But now wasn't the time to think about such things.

If you say so. Anyway, this sword has two abilities. First, it can weaken the barrier of anything it touches. Second, it can absorb a weapon's durability to the point of crippling it. If anything, it only makes this sword stronger.

That sounded powerful, especially on a swordbreaker. It made for the perfect combination.

It definitely sounds promising...

I didn't think we'd be going up against Fanatix, said Forlund. *But it should still work. That said, I don't know how much durability it will drain.*

Still, we have a chance now.

Forlund nodded. "Let us advance."

Yes, let's do this.

He grabbed me by the hilt and, while he didn't try to equip me, he faltered.

Forlund?!

"Urgh..."

A-are you okay?

Information overload...but I'll be fine. Let's focus on the attack.

R-right.

I was worried that he'd inadvertently triggered the goddess' curse, but it was just the analysis. What had he seen? I hoped he'd survive the battle so I could ask him later.

Forlund sighed and readied me. His mana wrapped around me until I was lifted from his hands. It was an odd sensation, having someone else move me telekinetically.

Forlund pulled his right hand back and opened his fingers, as if he were going to execute a palm strike. By now, I was floating over his right hand. He extended his left in front of him, as though to guide the path of my blade. Meanwhile, I Transmogrified into a rounder shape, cutting down on my wind resistance. Speed and spin were my top priorities, and I focused my energy on the tip of my blade, sharpening it. When I was done, I looked like a rapier without a hilt or guard. I'd tested this form out on the elephantman, so now it was pretty much perfect. But my transformation didn't stop there. Just when I thought it was over, Transmogrify activated again.

Wh-what?!

The area where my hilt used to be transformed into a cross. It was made of two silver blocks with the shape of an angel etched into it. I had never seen something like this before. Why had that happened? As I pondered this, something inside me said, "Worry not." It wasn't a voice exactly, but I could feel something reassuring me. Whatever it was, it was on my side. Both the cross and that presence must have come from Holy Order, reacting to Fanatix.

All right, good to see we're on the same page. Let's do this together.

"Are you all right, Teacher?"

Don't worry. I'm fine.

"I see. I'm prepared on my side."

Got it.

Forlund was rubbing off on me. I felt connected to him somehow, and I wondered if that had something to do with Beloved of the God Sword. Maybe it allowed him to connect better with swords or something.

CLASH OF THE TITANS

I watched with consternation as Urslars' aura grew redder and redder, waiting for our opening.

No...not yet...

"......"

Bracing was taking a huge toll on Forlund. The veins under his forehead pulsed and his hands tightened. But the man in black gritted his teeth and endured it. And he would continue to endure it until we achieved victory. Suddenly, he reminded me of Fran.

We watched and waited until our opportunity finally came. One of Urslars' attacks finally knocked Velmeria to the ground and, when she tried to get up, his gravitational pressure pinned her back down.

This was our first and final chance.

Now! I shouted.

"Here goes, Teacher!"

Forlund's palm exploded with mana, rocketing me through the air.

Ooooooh!

I opened a Dimension Gate into the air above Velmeria, although not *directly* above her. I needed to adjust for acceleration, after all.

I went faster and faster, picking up the speed I would need to damage Fanatix. I used Flame spells, Wind spells, Thunder spells, Timespace spells, Flame Control,

Air Control, everything in my arsenal to accelerate even more. I even took advantage of the Gravity Pressure as I approached.

Harder. Faster.

Weight Inflation, Vibrofang, even Dark and Light Elemental Blades. Dark was effective against an opponent's psyche, so it might give me the edge to trigger Cannibalize, while Light was even more advantageous. One look at Velmeria told me that she had high resistances against the four basic elements and their compounds. But Light was a rare enough element that it might get through her defenses. And that wasn't all.

I mimicked Fanatix's Mana Thruster to further increase my speed.

At times, it felt like I was losing control. I was using all these skills and spells on top of being pushed by telekinesis. Typically, I would've been thrown off course in an instant, but the telekinetic rail—which was more like a pipe at this point—kept me on the path. My durability dropped drastically from the recoil, but that was all part of the plan. Forlund was putting his life on the line, so it was the least I could do.

Raaaaah!

Velmeria saw me and was about to react...but she couldn't.

Forlund was right behind her.

The instant he launched me, I had opened another Dimension Gate so he could ambush her. Even if she managed to react to my attack, she wouldn't have time to avoid him too. It was too small a chance to even be called an opening, but Forlund didn't waste it. He got to work on holding her down immediately—thrusting his swordbreaker forward and catching Fanatix in its teeth.

Under normal circumstances, Velmeria would have broken free easily, but Urslars' gravity field was pinning her down, and it would take more than a swing to break free of the Demon Wolf's Jaw—especially when Forlund was putting his life on the line to hold her.

"Gaaaaah!"

"You're not getting away!"

Velmeria struggled against him, but it was too late.

Oaaaaaaah!

By now, I was a speeding bullet. I pierced right through Fanatix, straight into Forlund's sword and arm. His swordbreaker drained Fanatix's durability while Holy Order's energy covered me, neutralizing the mad sword's mana. Between them, they whittled down the Godsword's defenses to nothing.

Forlund was thrown back by the attack, spraying blood in the air. He had a smile on his lips when our eyes met, but unfortunately, I didn't have time to check up on him.

EEEEEEEEEEEEEGGGGGGH!

Someone was screaming. Maybe me. Maybe Fanatix. Maybe both of us. The influx of mana was too great.

Crap! Crap, crap, crap!
EEEEEEEEEEEEEEEEERRRRRGH!
So much mana!
It's hot!
I'm burning up!
I'm burning up from the inside!
The fire is splitting me open!
GRAAAAAAAAAAAAAAARGH!
I'm going to throw up!

It felt like a swarm of bugs were crawling under my skin, into my head, within my insides. It felt like my mind was being molded into something different. Suddenly, I was terrified.

WAAAAAAAAAAAAAAARGH!
Help! Someone help me! Please!
I'm breaking! Falling apart...!
Gaaaargh...
CRASH!

The sound of something breaking.

What was th—

WAAAAAAAAAAAAAAAAAAAAAAAAAAAAAAA AAAAAAAAAAAARGH!

Something black poured out from inside me.

Hot. Cold. Hurt. Pain. The blackness covered everything in sight, consuming it. But somehow, I knew it was a part of me. Part of what made me myself.

Eat.

Aaaargh...!

Eat.

The black thing was talking.

Aaaagh...?

Eat. Eat!

What...? Gaaaaah!

Eat?

Eat! Devour everything!

Devour...everything...?

This thing wasn't me, but it was part of me.

Who are you? What are you?

But it ignored me. Instead, it kept ordering me to satisfy its appetite.

That's when I remembered something. At the end of my fight against the elephantman, I'd heard a strange voice. This must be the same thing. That voice had finally come to the surface.

Heed my call! Offer thyself to me! Yield thyself to me!

Its voice rang in my mind—black, malicious, and repulsive.

Devour everything! Heaven and earth, gods and demons, man and beast, everything!

The voice was dripping with violent hunger. It wanted to devour, consume, eat. To eat flesh, drink blood, swallow the earth, bite the heavens. For some reason, I knew it could do it all.

Urgh!

Rage surged through me.

You want me...to eat it all?

Yes! Devour everything!

How dare you! You want me to eat everything?! Eat people?! Fran?! *Out of the question! I'll protect her from everything, even myself if I have to! If you want to get to her, you'll have to kill me first!*

I didn't know what I was thinking. I couldn't tell which thoughts were mine and which weren't.

Eat!

Aaaaaaaaaah!

EAT!

AAAARGH! SHUT UP! SHUT THE HELL UP!

Rage chased away the pain and disgust.

Obey me! Why won't you obey?!

I said, SHUT UP!

...!

Somehow, the voice fell completely silent.

Although the creature wasn't gone, I knew it was startled by my resistance. Having lost most of its strength, it retreated back inside me.

I guess I'm safe...for now.

That's when a shrill voice started talking, grating at my ears.

Hee hee hee! We were wondering what could've possibly eaten us up! You're something else, aren't you?

No!

I knew who this voice was. What it was. After all, we were both discarded Godswords.

Fanatix?

Hee hee! Your guess is as good as ours! We are us! But if you say that's who we are, then maybe it's true! But boy, you're keeping one hell of a pet inside you!

Every time Fanatix spoke, its voice changed. Male, then female. Young, then old.

Fanatix was inside of me now. I probably consumed it when Cannibalize activated, but the pain had kept me from noticing. This was the first time I recognized something that I Cannibalized, and the realization made me sick.

Hurk...!

Ga ha ha ha! You used to be human, didn't you? My deepest condolences!

Wh-what...?

You'll break one day! Man's not supposed to live inside a sword! You'll break just like us! We guarantee it!

No, I won't!

You can't help it! We looked inside you, you see? And you are definitely losing it! *I bet you'll end up killing your user!*

No! Stop talking!

Ga ha ha! Ugh! What the...?!

As Fanatix laughed, it suddenly started choking.

What the hell is this?!

It sounded afraid now, as if it found something it wasn't expecting inside of me. The P.A., the remnant of Cherubim, was using Holy Order's powers to absorb Fanatix's mind.

Why would something like this be here...?! And this disgusting power...Holy Order! What is it doing here?! Aaah, we get it! You absorbed its power from that shard! I should destroy you—eeeeeek!

Fanatix shrieked in pain.

Stop it! You can't eat us! We're *supposed to eat* you! *You won't get rid of us! Not like thiiiiiiiis!*

As the voice faded into oblivion, the nausea disappeared too. Eventually, there wasn't a trace of either one.

Is it over?

No one answered. I thought P.A. might start talking to me, but she remained silent. Still, her presence was stronger now. Absorbing Fanatix and Holy Order, along with all their powers, seemed to strengthen her. If I kept using Cannibalize, maybe she would come back.

For now, though, I should probably worry about myself. When I came to, I was in quite the state. My blade was cracked and falling apart, and I recovered even more slowly than when I fought Aschtner with the Divine element. But at least I *was* recovering. My durability was going up instead of down. Still, I barely survived that encounter...

But never mind me. What happened to Velmeria?!

I scanned the area. Had she finally stopped rampaging?

Where is she...? There!

Velmeria was lying on the ground. Her body had returned to its humanoid shape, and I could make out the faint rise and fall of her chest. She was alive, but barely. All that overwhelming mana had left her body. Her left arm had exploded along with Fanatix, while the whole right half of her body was torn to shreds. At least the bleeding had stopped, and her body was regenerating itself. With the correct medical attention, she should survive.

Urslars was on the other side of her. He was also lying on the ground, but only because his mana was exhausted. He wasn't wounded.

Urslars?

"Teacher? That you?"

Tired as he was, he could still talk.

You're not going to go berserk, are you?

"All thanks to you..."

We had avoided the worst. I just hoped my temporary partner was okay.

Forlund!

He was lying some distance away, and I used what little energy I had left to fly over to him. It was a struggle, and my hilt kept hitting the ground.

Oh no...

Forlund was a mess, to put it lightly. The flesh down the right side of his body had been cleaved away from his collarbone to his ribs, exposing the organs and bones beneath. His left arm was blown to pieces, and there was nothing left from the elbow down. The ground beneath him was dark and damp with blood.

"Urgh..."

But he was still alive. His left lung was still taking in air, and his heart was beating faintly. Cannibalizing Fanatix had replenished my mana, so I quickly rushed to heal him.

Forlund! Forlund!

"I'm...all right."

The worst was over. Forlund got to his feet and the bleeding slowing down to a trickle. If he was going in excruciating pain, he didn't let it show. Instead, he summoned a few more swords to aid his recovery. They probably came with Healing and Regenerative Skills. I guess he was prepared for this near-death scenario.

I'm glad to see you're okay.

Yes. I got to talk to a departed friend of mine.

I guess the life left him enough that he went to the other side at some point. If our angles had been even slightly different, I could have killed him. Velmeria too. They were both very lucky.

As I was talking to Forlund, Urslars got up and went to Velmeria's side. Gaia was still in its unleashed state.

Urslars, wait! You don't have to kill her! She's no longer a threat!

"Wasn't planning to. Watch."

The big man meant what he said. I didn't feel any murderous intent from him, so I waited and watched. Urslars raised Gaia over Velmeria.

"Smile of the Land."

Warm mana poured out of Gaia, embracing Velmeria. Her wound-stricken body was healed, and her complexion improved. Whatever that was, it was stronger than a Greater Heal. Gaia wasn't just a weapon of mass destruction. It could heal as well as harm. I guess that meant that Urslars had some way to heal himself when he went berserk.

"Uhh..."

"You all right, young lady?"

"Where...am I...?"

Velmeria was herself again. Her mind was intact, so it hadn't been assimilated into Fanatix. The Godsword must have released all the minds it held captive when it was destroyed. I guess Fanatix didn't have the ability to fully assimilate the minds it absorbed. If it did, it wouldn't need to drug its victims.

"Looks like you don't remember much of what happened," Urslars said. "That's all right. Just sleep for now."

"Ah..."

Velmeria quickly fell back to sleep. Although she survived, the experience had put a huge amount of stress on her mind and body. Even asleep, she still looked distressed. Whatever she was dreaming about, it wasn't good.

Urslars, can your Healing spell fix drug withdrawal?

"Withdrawal? I don't think so. It just heals wounds."

So, how did Velmeria wake up? She should be in withdrawal by now.

After all, that's exactly what Garrus was going through. And, since they were both given the same drugs, Velmeria's revival seemed strange.

A dwarf friend of mine is still unconscious after being poisoned by drugs.

"Uh-huh. I think it's because he had more of it over a longer period of time."

I see.

Garrus was kept under for a long time. Meanwhile, Velmeria had a huge dose all at once, which was probably why she wasn't going through withdrawal. The drug hadn't had a chance to accumulate.

"You guys saved the day," Urslars said, bowing his head. "Thank you."

His body was covered with wounds, and although they'd stopped bleeding, they hadn't started to heal. I guess his mana and life force were just too spent for that. Even worse, the Mad Ogre state seemed to have progressed even further. I couldn't even imagine how much stress that put on his mind.

"She was tough," he said. "I wouldn't have made it without you two."

We could say the same. Things look bad now, but it would've been worse if you weren't around.

Around us, the plaza looked more like the remains

of an ancient, ruined city than the present-day capital of Granzell. Half of the noble district was leveled, and its mansions reduced to little more than rubble. What's more, half of the beautiful palace—the hallmark of the capital—had been destroyed too. The common districts and the slums hadn't escaped unscathed either, as the fanatic soldiers' self-destruction made sure of that. This might've been the greatest calamity to ever hit the capital.

Still, we wouldn't have defeated Fanatix without you.

"Indeed," Forlund said.

"I guess we're even, then." Urslars sighed, scratching his head. "Still, I think we fought a little too hard. We should leave the country while we still can."

Huh? What are you doing?

Urslars put Gaia back in its sheath, walked over to Velmeria, and lifted her over his shoulder.

"I'm taking this young lady with me."

Hold on a second! Why?

But Forlund seemed to agree with him. "It's for the sake of the kingdom."

I still didn't understand.

"This battle has ruined a good chunk of the capital," Urslars explained. "And I had a good deal to do with it. But arresting me won't help fix it."

Between him and Forlund, I soon began to understand. Urslars' very existence too much for *any* country to deal with. The government might hold him responsible for the destruction, but that created its own set of problems. The death penalty was out of the question. Mad Ogre Form would trigger if it sensed that Urslars' life was in danger, and the same went for suicide.

They couldn't enslave him for the same reason. Even if Urslars could hold back, I doubted the government would want a ticking time bomb on their hands. And what a time bomb he was. If he exploded, he could wipe several cities off the map with ease. Any politician who wanted to take that risk was either stupid, suicidal, or both.

What about sending him to fight enemy states? No, that would only enemy of the Adventurer's Guild. After all, the guild didn't participate in wars, and wouldn't appreciate anyone conscripting one of their S-Ranks. They would either have to crush the kingdom involved or risk losing face.

It was difficult to pin the blame on Urslars to begin with. This whole incident was caused by Marquis Aschtner's coup. A lot of adventurers lost their lives, and the government had failed to see it coming. Depending on your point of view, Urslars had saved the kingdom by defeating Aschtner's trump card. So, if the government tried to blame Urslars, the Adventurer's Guild would come to his aid, and the kingdom would be at a stark disadvantage in the conflict that would follow.

Granzell's neighbors would also be paying attention to what happened here. They would know Urslars possessed a Godsword and might suspect Granzell of wanting to use it for themselves. Of course, Granzell could demand the Godsword in exchange for damages, or just take Gaia after putting Urslars to death. Despite how unlikely those scenarios were, the possibility alone would cause diplomatic problems.

Neither could they say that Urslars was a hero who saved the country from Marquis Aschtner's plot without giving the impression that Granzell was trying to keep an S-Rank to itself. Their neighbors might even begin to suspect that Granzell was plotting something—that they were keeping a superweapon around for a reason—and that would be the worst scenario of all.

Urslars was untouchable, and a problematic character for any politician to deal with. The best anyone could do was avoid him entirely. Even the Beast King left him to his own devices.

The only course left was for him to leave Granzell, and for the country to issue a deportation notice. Any kingdom would do the same to the adventurer nicknamed Friendly Fire, and Friendly Fire didn't mind wandering the world as a result.

Anyone else would have been enslaved or sentenced to death, but Urslars' situation was unique. However, the same could not be said of Velmeria. Even if she *was* the count's illegitimate daughter, that wouldn't help her much. After all, she was also the one responsible for most of the damage. The government would do whatever it could to bring her to justice. But honestly? I didn't think she was to blame for any of this. The people here might disagree, but I felt nothing but sympathy for her. She got dragged into a forty-year plot by a Godsword and a marquis against her will. Anyone would have struggled to escape their influence. So, in the end, I felt oddly at peace with the idea of Urslars taking her away.

Take care of her.

"Don't worry," Urslars smiled. "I won't do anything bad. I have a sinking feeling that this might be fate."

I really wish Fran could see her before you leave.

"We're on a tight schedule, so that probably won't happen. But we'll see each other again."

Fran would be disappointed when she woke up.

Where are you headed?

"I was originally headed to Goldicia to track down Theraclede. That's the perfect place for her to lay low, and we can make a living killing monsters there."

Theraclede's in Goldicia?

"Chances are he is, yeah."

Goldicia was always looking for powerful warriors to take care of the S-Threat monsters prowling about the continent. They didn't care about your past there, which made it the world's safest haven for criminals. But Urslars' friend was in charge of things there, and there were a lot of drakes and halflings around too. It was the best place for Velmeria right now.

I see.

"We'll be going, then," said Urslars. "If I stick around any longer, the guards might come for me."

Yeah.

"Teacher." Urslars nodded. "Forlund."

"Farewell," Forlund said.

Be seeing you.

Urlsars left quickly, though not at full speed. He would've made quite the picturesque escape if he weren't carrying Velmeria on his shoulder. The gates were on the other side of town, but I was sure the S-Rank adventurer would figure something out. I had known he was strong before, but today had really driven it home. Urslars was monstrous. From where I was, the titan's powers were ridiculous.

So, what will you do now, Forlund?

"I will report to the guildmaster."

I see. I'll come with you. Actually, I'd appreciate it if you would take me along. Don't want people to think I'm some kind of flying sword.

"Very well."

His wounds were mostly healed, so Forlund put me on his back and walked toward the gravity-flattened palace.

SIDE: ARISTEA

This was an emergency.

"This feeling...a Godsword!"

I felt it unleashing its powers somewhere on the continent. All Godsmiths had this ability to search for Godswords, so I couldn't miss one unleashing its powers. This time, there were two of them.

One was the Land Sword Gaia, wielded by Urslars—I knew its mana all too well. But I couldn't tell what the other one was, which meant this was a Godsword I had never touched before. Its energy was strange, and clearly twisted in some way. Maybe it had suffered damage in the battle and couldn't unleash its true powers.

"I'll figure it out when I see it!"

I had to go. This was my life's calling, my mission, and the Godswords were *definitely* in Granzell. But someone stopped me before I could leave.

"Ari? Where do you think you're going?"

A woman with blonde hair, white skin, a slender body, and pointed ears—the trademarks of an elf.

"Wynalin...! When did you get here?!"

Despite her soft and gentle appearance, I couldn't lie to this woman. She was also the only person in the world that I didn't dare to cross.

"This is my house," she said. "I know when someone is skulking around."

"But I used a tool to hide my presence!"

Wynalin raised her eyebrows. "Did you, now? You don't seem hidden to me. It must be a dud."

"Godsmiths don't make duds!" I complained. "You high elves are just too strong!"

This woman was no ordinary elf. Wynalin was one of the few high elves, reputed to be the strongest of all races. And she was a famous one, at that.

No one knew how many high elves there were. They didn't often meddle with the everyday affairs of ordinary people, but there were a few who did, and Wynalin was one of them. Historian Willow Magnus was another. Wandering botanist Wiggan Wiggan was the third. It was purely coincidental that all their names started with "W." Apparently, they were all born during a period where it was a popular way to name your children. Given how long elves lived, I had no idea when that was.

High elves with last names used to be nobles. I say "used to" because their countries no longer existed. These kingdoms had probably tried to win the high elves over by giving them high statuses, but it didn't work. Some say Wiggan's last name came about because he couldn't even be bothered to come up with a proper name. Either way, the fact that these countries no longer existed proved that the high elves weren't interested in politics. If they had been, then they could have easily prevented those countries from disappearing.

A lot of stories circulated around the three high elves. We knew for certain that Willow Magnus and Wiggan Wiggan traveled the world—researching and submitting their findings to their guilds now and again. Wynalin, on the other hand, had permanent residence.

She was famous for the two positions she held. First, she was a member of the Seven Sages—a group of people as strong as S-Rank adventurers. Of course, the Seven Sages didn't really call themselves that—it was something that others had come up with. Besides, there were only two mages among the Seven Sages.

The group came about after the meteoric rise of the Adventurer's Guild, when various organizations and kingdoms recognized it was a threat. In the end, the Seven Sages were the only seven people strong enough to counteract that, and the name gave the public an impression of intelligence and calm—the opposite of rough and tumble adventurers.

It was foolish, but the Seven Sages were not to be taken lightly. After all, three of them were Godsword wielders. One of them was a knight who held the First Godsword, Alpha, although not much more was known about them. There was also the Queen of the Night, who wielded the Mad Sword Berserk. The Queen of the Night wasn't an actual person, but an organization that ensured their Godsword's succession. Finally, there was the king of Phyllius, wielder of the Demon King Sword Diablos— although I had my doubts about that.

I didn't think that Diablos' master would be so public about it. The chances were more likely that royals were claiming to possess it to hide the real wielder's identity. Even a king could be a body double for the Godsword user, and I had a feeling that the true wielder was a member of the royal family whom they all claimed to be dead.

Of the remaining four Sages, three were kings of powerful kingdoms. The king of the magi, king of the insectoids, and king of the dwarves. I didn't know how strong they were. Their kingdoms were so powerful that no one dared to attack them, so they had never experienced war before. Chances were that they had all seen battle, but I certainly had never seen them fight.

Finally, there was the high elf Wynalin. I knew her powers well. A long time ago, we had explored a dungeon to collect materials. But, although she was a member of the Seven Sages, she was more famous for her *other* position as the Rector of the Academy of Magic.

The Academy had obtained special autonomy from the kingdom of Belioth, and gifted children were sent there from all over the world to learn magic. And Wynalin was its rector, because how could she not be? The high elf was the world's greatest ocean mage, after all.

Of course, there were other magic schools and academies, but when anyone talked about the "Academy of Magic," they meant Wynalin's.

"You still have lots of work, don't you?" she asked.

"I-I do."

"I'm heartbroken, Ari. I didn't think you'd go back on your word."

"Urgh..."

Wynalin and I had known each other for a long time, and I was currently staying at the Academy. It was one of the few places I could relax, and I'd taken up a position as a temporary smithing instructor. It was a simple job. All I needed to do was provide the young ones with a little bit of direction. I wasn't getting paid, but in exchange for accommodations and a position, I ran maintenance on their manatek and enchanted arsenal.

Honestly, it worked out pretty well for me. The Academy was always producing interesting manatek, and it was exciting to inspect them.

"A-all right, look," I started. "But I can't *leave* a Godsword like that."

"I suppose," Wynalin mused. "Godswords are very dangerous."

"Exactly."

"But the advanced classes need those weapon repairs."

"That is true..."

I couldn't make demands of her. She had taken good care of me since we were young. Also, I had seen her angry once and would rather not go through it again. Wynalin might *seem* soft and gentle, but that was mostly just for appearances. She wasn't a bad person, but a teacher needed a mask with her students. Beneath the mask, she was quite bold and willful.

"And the golems still need fixing," she went on. "We can't have our dueling classes without them."

"Surely you can figure something out! Maybe they can duel with you."

"Oh, all right. I'll let you off, just this once."

"I owe you one!"

"But I have some homework for you."

"H-homework?"

Don't tell me she's going to use this opportunity to make an unreasonable request...

"Yes. You know how I've been wanting you to introduce my dueling lecturer to the Beast King? Or Urslars?"

"That would be..."

Why would she need her lecturer to duel an S-Rank, anyway? Was she preparing them to fight the Evil One? But before I could tell her that it would be impossible, Wynalin backed off.

"Impossible, I know. So, I'll make a compromise."

"A compromise?"

"Yes. I want you to look for someone strong. They don't have to be as strong as those two, but at least a B-Rank, to put it in adventurer terms. Preferably someone who has a specialty comparable to A-Ranks."

"What? That's impossible!"

Anyone with an A-Rank specialty would already *be*

an A-Rank. If nothing else, they would have to be at the top of B-Rank.

"I'm sure you'll figure something out," said Wynalin.

"No!"

"Then will you talk to the Beast King and Urslars for me?"

"Fine..."

There's no winning against this woman.

"I'll take care of it."

"Promise me," she said. "I don't leave this place often, so I don't really have any connections."

I suppose I could rely on the Beast King for this one. If not, I could commission manatek for the guild in exchange for an adventurer.

"You won't be able to hold a high-rank adventurer for long," I warned.

"I know that. It'll just take a week."

"And when should I bring them here?"

"Let me think...the sooner the better, so how about within five years?"

Fortunately, elves didn't see time in the same way as we did. Five years would be long enough to deal with her request. It even meant that I wouldn't have to think about it for a while, and that was just as well. After all, I had a Godsword to deal with.

To Granzell!

Reincarnated as a sword

5

Black Cat Saint

FORLUND AND I TALKED as we made our way to the palace.

Couldn't the government just retroactively issue a quest for Urslars? I asked. *Make it sound like they knew about the coup, and they commissioned him to take care of it, you know? It'd even protect their reputation.*

That was how it worked with Fran and the Beastman Nation, but Forlund shook his head.

Perhaps it would work with someone else, replied Forlund. *But things are different when it comes to that man.*

Because of his Godsword?

Because he specializes in mass destruction. All of the stories about him involve chaos and slaughter. Of course, that's commonplace on the battlefield, and there are many legends about heroes doing the same. But to actually hire Urslars...

It would make it sound like Granzell wanted to take advantage of his kingdom-crushing powers. Ordinarily, that wouldn't be an issue—if any of the other countries asked, they could just say the wandering berserker happened to be in town and they hired him on the spot. But Granzell's military already had to deal with the riots in Bulbola, and now there were riots in the capital. The last thing they wanted was to provoke a war. As long as the threat of Raydoss loomed in the north, they needed to maintain good relations with their neighbors.

Who knows what the kingdom would do with him? Forlund said. *But Urslars has already made his decision. Turning himself in would likely cause problems for Granzell. It is the simpler if he just leaves quietly.*

So that's it, huh?

Unfortunately, yes.

Forlund and Urslars had probably already considered any solution I could think of. After all, Urslars had been doing this for decades. He knew how to best deal with the situation.

Personally, I didn't think Urslars could be blamed for much of the destruction. I mean, he was basically fighting against a terrorist, capable of destroying the whole country.

Even if it was a force majeure, said Forlund. *He* did

attack the palace and lay waste to the noble district. Like it or not, those are crimes.

I liked Urslars, so I was probably biased. Perhaps it would help me to understand if we had an example back in Japan...

Let's say that one day, a terrorist in a giant robot attacked Tokyo. The JSDF was helpless to defend against its rockets and laser beams. Then, just as all hope seemed lost, another giant robot appeared to save the day! Robot Two defeated the terrorist bot, but it also destroyed the nearby districts and took hundreds of lives...

Yeah, that would be bad. Even if the pilot of Robot Two were on the side of humanity, some people would still throw rocks. The internet would burn him alive, and his supporters would be easily outnumbered by those who spoke against him.

Maybe I just couldn't get it because I came from modern Japan, but this world was different. A true monarchy, with kings and nobles. With all that considered, perhaps leaving without a word really was the best course of action. Either way, Urslars was probably miles away by now, so there was use worrying about him.

Anyway, let's see what I got from Cannibalize...whoa!

I couldn't stifle my scream when I looked at my stats. "Hrm?"

Sorry. It's nothing.

"All right."

I was a *lot* stronger than I'd expected. I had over 5000 MP—five times as much as before—and over 3000 durability. As broken as Fanatix was, it was still a Godsword. Perhaps this was the standard reward for Cannibalizing one.

But that wasn't all. I also had a new skill, Mana Supply, which allowed me to share my mana with my user. While Fran already drew from my mana pool, this skill would further reduce the cost of casting spells, greatly increasing its efficiency. It was nothing fancy, but it was definitely useful.

Soon, we saw Count Bayreeds directing some refugees into a hall, along with Erianthe and Colbert. Fran's aura was currently outside the capital, so it looked like Jet had managed to leave in time.

I would like to report to the count, said Forlund. *Do you mind?*

Not at all. You know Count Bayreeds?

I do. He is important to us adventurers. I've fought under his command several times.

I see. Go for it. I think you should tell him what happened, especially about Velmeria.

I didn't know whether the city was completely safe,

but with Fanatix destroyed, there was little reason to keep evacuating. More importantly, the count deserved to know what happened to his daughter.

When Forlund approached, Count Bayreeds was still in the middle of directing civilians. Erianthe was the first to notice Forlund, and she called out to him with a worried voice.

"Forlund, you're alive!"

"Yes."

After that, they all approached at once.

"So, what happened out there? It sounds like the fighting's stopped, but..."

"It's over."

"Urslars won?"

"Yes."

But Forlund was a man of so few words that it was difficult to give them a proper report. I ended up telling him what to say through telepathy. Fortunately, Fran had prepared me for that sort of thing.

"Urlslars won," Forlund said, following my lead. "Marquis Aschtner is defeated, and the soldiers under his command self-destructed."

Come on, you can do better than that! You're just giving them bullet points!

It's the best I can do. I'm not used to making long speeches.

I guess long sentences were too much for Forlund. At least he was trying.

"What happened to the girl Sir Urslars fought?" Bayreeds asked.

"He defeated her."

Bayreeds swallowed. "I see."

"And what about Urslars himself?" Erianthe asked.

"He left. To avoid complicating things."

As much as I would love to tell the count the truth, there were too many ears here. I felt bad for making him think that his daughter was dead, but he would have to bear with it for now.

"Forlund?"

"You sure you're all right?" Colbert said.

Meanwhile, Erianthe and Colbert looked perplexed at all the words coming out of Forlund's mouth. This unusually talkative man was a strange sight for them. Still, he pressed on, telling the count everything we knew. With this newfound information, they regrouped to discuss the evacuation and clean up. I figured they should be able to take care of the situation now.

All right. Can you take me to Fran now, Forlund?

"Right."

Forlund turned to walk away, but Erianthe stopped him.

"Wait! Where are you going? I was going to ask you to help."

"Can't."

Forlund shook his head and removed me from his back.

"Fran needs this."

Erianthe stared at me. "That sword..."

"What is it doing here?" Colbert asked in disbelief.

I couldn't blame them. There wasn't really a reasonable explanation for my being here!

Wait, I know! Forlund can tell them that Beloved of the Sword God—

But before Forlund could tell them my excuse, Colbert gazed toward the horizon.

"Master of Curry...you managed to protect Fran, in the end..."

Erianthe sniffled. "It is a miracle for his beloved student."

They seemed to have had the wrong idea. I wanted to tell them how wrong they were, but I couldn't afford to reveal my identity here. Forlund knew the truth, of course, but he kept his mouth shut, as was his style.

"......"

No excuses would come out of *his* lips.

"I'll be going."

"Of course," said Erianthe. "Make sure you get that sword to her."

Colbert held his tears. "Master of Curry...you were a blessing to the world!"

I appreciated the sentiment, I really did. But I wasn't dead! I wasn't a ghost on the battlefield! Still, Forlund left before I could clear things up with them. I'd need to get Fran to explain the situation later.

As we were on the way, I asked Forlund about something that had been on my mind.

So, what did you see when Beloved of the Sword God analyzed me?

Maybe I could recover a piece of my past life.

Forlund looked pensive. *Usually, the skill reveals a sword's maker and abilities. But this time, I saw a strange sight.*

Strange how?

Something led a man to a sword that emitted an ominous aura. The sword resembled you, but it differed in its details.

Wh-what did it look like?

Its blade was exactly like yours, but the crest on the pommel was different. Instead of a wolf, it was of a four-faced woman.

The Godsword Cherubim. I didn't know why it emitted

an ominous aura, but the sword was deemed dangerous enough for the gods to discard it. So, the man in the scene had to be…

Wh-what did the man look like? I asked.

Hmm…

What's wrong?

I only know he had black hair and black eyes. He was otherwise unimpressive. In fact, it was impressive how unimpressive he was.

I see…

It hurt…but now I knew for sure.

I think that was me.

You used to be human?

Yeah. I'm a human soul stuck inside a sword. But I have no idea who did this to me.

I knew the Godsmith Elmera was involved in making me, but maybe Forlund saw others in his vision.

What was it like? I asked. *Tell me everything you saw.*

You don't remember?

Not a bit.

I see. Unfortunately, I couldn't see much. My vision was hazy, like a mist hung over it.

I'll take anything you could make out.

Well, the first thing I saw were three beings.

Three beings?

The fact that he said "beings" instead of people implied that these were gods or angels. It wasn't a word you used lightly.

Strange visions only occur in analysis when a god, or their servants, are involved with the creation of a sword, Forlund explained. *If the analysis fails, I see a vision of the sword's creation instead.*

And you saw all that when you picked me up?

Normally, Forlund didn't have any visions; he just received the sword's data straight into his brain.

The vision was transmitted to the back of my mind, so it was hazy. I saw you converse with these gods—or their messengers.

Could you hear what we were talking about?

No. I only saw that you were smiling.

The vision didn't have audio. Still, this was the most I had discovered about my past so far.

Forlund told me everything he could about the vision. It took place in an undisclosed location with a strange white mist covering the ground and sky. Everyone there looked like they were floating in the air. The three beings were female, although their faces were veiled by shadow. They must've either been goddesses themselves, or their messengers.

I was brought before the sword, talked with them, and

was eventually sealed inside it. Forlund said I was smiling, so I must have consented to the process.

And then a strange thing happened, he said. *One of the goddesses placed her hand above you and extracted an image that hung in the air.*

What kind of image was it?

I didn't see you in it—just these gigantic square towers looming around whoever was watching. I think he was lying on the ground, and he must have been injured because there was blood on his body and his hands.

Were they memories of my death? I couldn't quite remember what happened. All I knew was that I was run over by a car. When I woke up, I was a sword.

There was also a scene where the observer was looking at a beautiful woman, and one where he held hands with a younger girl.

Scratch that. Maybe these weren't my memories at all. Then again, I couldn't remember anything from my past life, so who knew?

Then he was watching a box where a naked man and woman—

Wait! Stop!

Okay, that sounded familiar. I felt embarrassment suddenly, but this was the only lead I had...

Sorry about that. Go on.

"Indeed."

Forlund told me more about the image the goddess had summoned. There were memories of me eating, crying at a movie, being rejected by a woman. Also present were indecent and—let me be frank—lewd and sexual memories.

I couldn't remember any of that. From what Forlund said, it sounded like the gods had taken those memories out of me. That had to be why I couldn't remember anything when I arrived in this world. Forlund couldn't tell me any other details, but if I was smiling when I was sealed inside the sword, I must've agreed to it. But why did I still have memories of my death when I had forgotten everything else?

And then I saw the seals.

Seals?

Symbols which represent the gods. Each god has their own, and the three women had these seals on their bodies.

Apparently, he could make out the seals of the Goddess of Chaos, the Goddess of the Silver Moon, and the Goddess of the Nether.

So, the ones who made me were either goddesses or their messengers?

Probably.

Maybe I should look into who they were. The only thing I knew about these goddesses were their names.

But you really are an amazing sword, said Forlund.

Yeah? I mean not to brag, but I am a discarded Godsword, so I guess I'm stronger than most.

Perhaps, but "Godsword" is bestowed with the powers of a single deity, and three *goddesses bestowed their powers on you. This is unheard of. What in the world were you made for?*

That's what I'd like to know. Really. Who am I? What am I?

I don't know who made me, or for what purpose. But the more I thought about it, the more afraid I was.

Ten minutes after we left Erianthe, I guided Forlund to Fran and the others at the capital's outer walls, where the Adventurer's Guild had evacuated their non-combatants.

Fran and Garrus were sleeping on mats laid out on the ground, while Eiworth was sitting next to them on a stool that I wondered where it had come from. A broken Fanatix replica was in his hand, and he was busy inspecting it. In his other hand was a bundle of documents that he referred to frequently. Some of the pages had drawings of the Fanatix replica on them, so they must have been related to his research. I hoped he would share what he learned with us later.

Should I just leave you here? Forlund asked.

Yeah. Thanks for everything.

Forlund placed me next to Fran.

Fran? Fran.

"Zzz..."

There was no response. Fran was still fast asleep. I Identified her and saw that nothing was physically wrong. She was just exhausted and needed to rest. Meanwhile, Forlund was explaining the situation to Eiworth.

Eiworth looked up at him. "Is that you, Hundred Blades? Is it over?"

"Yes."

"I see. And how did it go? Did Friendly Fire win?"

"Yes."

The old man showed his guile by asking Forlund simple yes or no questions. Stellia listened but didn't interrupt. Forlund should be able to handle Eiworth.

Nice work, Jet.

Woof!

I commended our direwolf for a job well done. He let out a soft whine from the shadows, where he was lying next to Fran.

What is it? I asked. *Are you still hurt?*

Rumble. He was hungry. It was only natural. Jet hadn't eaten anything the whole day. He did well not to take what he could in the chaos like a looter.

Oh, all right. Hide me from the others, boy.

"Arf!"

Jet leapt out of the shadows and created a curtain with Shadow Magic. When it was in place, I took out some extra spicy curry and placed it in front of him. Jet had earned it for protecting Fran while I was away.

Don't spill it.

"Woof woof!"

"What was that?" Eiworth turned his head. "Now, where did that come from? From the shadows, given the presence of Shadow Magic..."

Fortunately, he didn't suspect me of anything. Forlund did, but then again, he already knew about me.

"Arf arf!"

Jet's maw turned red from the giant serving of super-hot curry and Fran stirred in her sleep. She sniffed the air, ears twitching, and finally opened her eyes slowly.

"Smells like curry," she mumbled.

"Woof!"

"Jet...no fair..."

The smell of curry alone was enough to wake her up when nothing else would. It really did have a powerful hold on her. Or maybe it was just her appetite.

"Impossible," Eiworth gawked. "My Awakening potion was supposed to keep her under for days..."

Days?!

Fran's love for curry was great enough to cause a miracle.

"Teacher... Curry..."

Fran! There are people here!

Hm. Curry.

All right, all right. Here you go.

"Hm..."

I produced another giant serving of curry and placed it in front of her, careful to make it look like she'd taken it out of her own inventory. Her curry came with tonkatsu and karaage—popular breakfast items, as far as Fran was concerned. She moved the spoon sleepily to her mouth.

"Munch munch."

"Ruff ruff."

"Wh-what is it that you're eating?" Eiworth asked.

He was staring at the spicy, strange-to-him dish with deep curiosity. For a man of science like Eiworth, this was a subject of great interest. He was also probably starving after that huge fight. Once he started sniffing the delectable aroma, he couldn't ignore it for long.

"T-tell me. Is that good?"

"Hm. Really good."

"Indeed?"

Fran turned away to avoid his gaze and shield her curry—intent on keeping it to herself.

Fran, maybe we should share a plate with him.
Hrm.
Come on, don't pout. Eiworth helped us a lot today.
"Fine..."

Fran wasn't happy about it, but she gave Eiworth a small serving. Small enough to confirm exactly how she felt about him.

"Here."

"Excellent! Let's see..." Eiworth inspected the curry, took a few whiffs, and dug right in. "Ah! How interesting! But delicious!"

He scarfed it down, showing exactly how sensitive his taste buds really were.

"Eight spices...no, nine? Broth made of pig monster bones. Four vegetables."

And just like that, he reverse-engineered my recipe. Maybe it was because of all his work with potions. Either way, he could make a killing selling these now!

"Don't worry, I won't spread your recipe around," he said. "But you won't mind if I cook some for private consumption, will you?"

Eiworth was hooked. I couldn't imagine this old man cooking curry in his kitchen, but Fran was happy to evangelize it. Meanwhile, Forlund was staring jealously at Eiworth, so we had to give him a portion too.

"Hm."

"Thanks."

A large plate. Forlund was *definitely* on Fran's good list. He gave her a deep bow and started eating. He seemed to like it too, because he cleaned the whole plate in a flash.

As everyone was feasting, I filled Fran in on what happened while she was asleep.

Hrmph.

What's wrong?

I was useless. Didn't do anything.

It couldn't be helped. Even Forlund had trouble looking for an opening against Velmeria.

Fran pouted. *But you and Forlund still got to fight.*

I paused for a moment. *That was only because of Forlund's special abilities. It's a good thing he has them, but he still almost died out there.*

Teacher...

What's up?

Is Forlund strong?

Y-yeah.

Oh...

Was Fran jealous because I praised him? A whirlwind of emotions was certainly going through her. Disappointment at not fighting a powerful enemy.

Powerlessness at not being able to help. Jealousy at my teaming up with Forlund. And finally, anxiety.

I'm weak... I couldn't fight until the end. Not like Forlund...

She was comparing herself to him. I knew the feeling well. If Fran started comparing me to other Godswords, then I'd be uncomfortable too.

He's trustworthy, and his telekinetic abilities are useful. That much is true.

Hm...

But you're still the best for me, Fran. I lost count of all the times I wished you were there. I'm so much weaker without you.

You're not weak!

I mean, I'm stronger than the average sword, sure. But I'm stronger when you're with me. You understand me better than anyone, and you know how to use my powers best.

I wasn't trying to console her. I'd thought about this a lot.

That's why I need to get stronger. To become a sword that's worthy of you.

Fran wanted to raise the status of Black Cats everywhere by breaking the curse and allowing all of them to Evolve. That meant that at some point, we had to fight an S-Threat Fiend—an enemy of titanic strength, like the ones I saw today.

For now, it was a distant dream. But I knew Fran wouldn't give up. Besides, she still had some growing up to do, so I was sure that she'd make it one day. And, when that day came, I needed to be powerful enough to keep serving her. I'd gained a lot of mana from cannibalizing Fanatix, so I should get some new skills and train them up too.

We're a lot stronger now, Fran. But we'll have to keep going if we're to beat every enemy we come across. You and me both.

Fran nodded. *Hm.*

I guess that was painfully obvious to her.

We'll get stronger together, I told her.

Okay! So, do we start training?

Yep. I need more crystals, and you need EXP. Lots of it. Fortunately, I know the perfect place to train.

Where?

The place where it all began for me. The Demon Wolf's Garden. I've always wanted to go back there. Might as well train while we're at it.

Hm! I'll get a lot stronger, she said. *Then I can fight with you to the end!*

But we would have to wait until things settled down in the capital.

Fran finished her curry while Eiworth and Forlund wrapped up their conversation.

"So Friendly Fire beat the count's daughter, and now both of them are on the run to avoid complications?" Eiworth asked.

"Yes," Forlund said.

"I see... Well, considering that Friendly Fire turned up, and the destruction was mostly in the noble district, I'd say we got off easy," Eiworth said nonchalantly.

E-easy? Most of the noble district had been converted into vacant lots and there was a giant hole in the side of the palace! But Forlund seemed to agree.

"Urslars caused a lot of destruction."

Eiworth scoffed. "And it could have been *much* worse. The whole capital could've been obliterated. Instead, only a single district was destroyed. It could have been a much larger area."

The capital had managed to avoid the worst, but things were still really bad. Lots of people were wounded, and many more had lost their homes. No one but Eiworth could talk about it so nonchalantly without caring who heard.

Stellia sighed, her countenance grim. "I wonder what's going to happen to the capital now. The coup caused a lot of chaos, and a lot of injured and dead too."

Fran got up. *Let's go, Teacher.*

Go where?

She had only just woken up. Did she really want to start training *now*? Even if she were conscious, she really needed her rest.

To save the wounded.

Fran's spirit was still on fire, and she had recovered at least some of her mana while she was asleep. Now, she had a look of unwavering resolve.

Hmm...

But relief work was tiring—both physically and magically. It wasn't a job for someone who was still recovering. But Fran wanted to help the wounded, and I wasn't about to stop her as long as she was able to do it.

All right. Let's head back to Erianthe's.

That should be where most of the injured were. There were probably still plenty of wounded people out in the city, but the guild and knight brigade should be able to take care of that. There was one problem, however.

What should we do about Garrus...? I asked.

We'll put him on top of Jet.

I don't think that's going to work.

Garrus was still weak and unconscious. We managed to evacuate him here, but moving him again would take its toll on his body.

"Hrm..."

"What is it, Fran?" Stellia asked.

"I want to go help the wounded, but I can't leave Garrus here by himself."

"Old Garrus is still beat up," said Stellia, giving a worried sigh. "And who knows what's going to happen once he wakes up..."

Could they really charge Garrus with something? He might have been manipulated with drugs, but he was still involved with the production of Fanatix replicas, and those things caused a *lot* of destruction. Would they consider the extenuating circumstances? Or would they immediately impose a heavy penalty on him? I was no expert in law and politics, so I had no idea.

"Anyway, your quest is still in effect," said Stellia, "so the Adventurer's Guild won't abandon him. We'll take care of him, I promise."

"That's right," Forlund said.

Eiworth was nodding too. "The state won't be so stupid as to punish him in the midst of so much chaos. And they'll probably let him off easy so he can work for them."

That was a good point.

"Besides," he went on, "my employers want me to keep him safe, and I'm the only one who can deal with his withdrawal symptoms. So, you have nothing to fear."

Fran, we don't have to trust Eiworth, but we can trust Forlund and Stellia. Let the guild take care of Garrus.

Fran paused, silently glaring at Eiworth. "All right," she said at last. "Take care of him for me, Stellia."

"You got it. You get to helping everyone else."

After that, we headed to Erianthe's location and asked her where the injured were. There were several field hospitals where doctors, mages, and alchemists ran to and fro, helping the wounded as best they could. All of them looked exhausted, but they drank mana potions and chugged along.

Come on, Teacher!
Hang on. We have to talk to the one in charge first.
Okay.

If a child suddenly appeared and started healing patients, it would only cause confusion. Fran talked to the receptionist. When she told her that she could use Healing Magic, the receptionist brought Fran to see her superior.

A court doctor was overseeing this field hospital. They were experts, specializing in medicine, Healing Magic, and alchemy. Apparently, the king had ordered all of his court doctors aside from the head physician to aid the relief effort.

"Excuse me," the receptionist said.

"Hrm? What happened now?"

"Nothing, sir. But this girl says she wants to help."

"Oh? An adventurer, are you? Can you use Healing Magic?"

Fran nodded. "Hm."

"Wonderful!" The man beamed. "We need all the healers we can get right now! What spells can you use?"

"Up to Greater Heal?"

"Wh-what? But that's a Recovery spell. Are you sure?"

"Mm."

"Even better!"

The court doctor had an air of professional pride, but rejoiced when he heard what Fran could do. He knew that this was now time for territorial bickering.

"Can you tend to the critically wounded first?" he asked. "We'll get you all the mana potions you need."

"Got it."

We went around the field hospitals, healing all the patients we could. Although our battles had exhausted most of our mana, Cannibalizing Fanatix had filled me back up again, so Fran was able to heal patients so quickly that it surprised the court doctors. They were so worried that she would exhaust herself, so they kept pushing mana potions on her.

By the time we were done, we must have healed over five hundred people—including the ones we pulled from the rubble on our way to each field hospital. When they were stable, a lot of the patients stayed behind to help. Some even clasped their hands in prayer when they saw Fran again. She was acknowledged as the little Black Cat who risked her life to heal the wounded. Fran didn't have time to talk to them, but she waved back casually.

Right to the end, her desire to help overwhelmed her exhaustion. She was happy that people were thanking her, but even happier that she could save them.

You sure you don't need a break?

"Yeah!"

At midnight, Fran finally made her way back to the guild. She wanted to continue helping, but the court doctors insisted that she get some rest. The critically wounded were all taken care of, and there were plenty of people around to maintain the field hospitals. Fran no longer needed to push herself.

We helped a lot of people today.

"Hm!"

"Hey, you!"

As Fran was about to enter the guild, three men stepped out in front of her. I wondered what kind of chump would attack her without concealing their presence, but apparently they had business with her.

"You must be the Black Cat healer!" The small pudgy man in the center spoke with an arrogant voice. "You use your Healing Magic to heal the people, do you not?"

"Hm."

"Then rejoice! I am here to make you a retainer for my barony! From now on, you will use your powers for my good!"

It was an invitation? Although, considering this guy's attitude, I didn't think anyone would be happy to accept it. The baron seemed a little less than noble.

"You've been healing all these people for free!" he said. "Well, you won't have to stoop that low anymore! Nobles and merchants will pay handsomely for your services under me."

"What do you mean?" Fran asked.

"I mean you are to heal whoever I tell you to heal and no one else! Many want a powerful healer, and they are willing to pay for it. Under me, you will get the highest price out of even the most hardened merchant. But rest assured, you will be compensated fairly."

"And what about the people who can't pay?"

"The poor? Ah, the world won't miss them. With their empty wallets, they barely change the world at all!"

What an absolute idiot. He was trying to buy Fran out with money? If he had done his due diligence, he would've known that she refused to take any reward from her patients. What's more, his "invitation" sounded more like a stuck-up command, and he didn't even seem to notice it. If you looked up "idiot noble" in the dictionary, this man's face would show right up. Even his bodyguards looked tired of his behavior, but the fool didn't notice that either.

"You'll never have to waste your time like you did today ever again."

"......"

Fran's anger was silently mounting. If all the noble did was make light of her with his invitation, she would've ignored it and gone along on her way. She was tired, and he wasn't worth her time. But saying that the poor deserved to die really crossed the line.

I'm going to kill him, said Fran.

Wait! Stop! I understand, but you can't kill him!

He said helping people was a waste of time. Everyone was so happy when I helped them. It meant they could help others...and he called that a waste!

This was very bad. Fran's anger was reaching critical mass. She felt like this noble was tainting something she held dear. If he kept it up, she might really cut him down. Of course, he didn't notice the change in her mood, but his guards were white as sheets. Weak as they were, they could feel Fran's urge to kill. And, if anything happened to their master, they would be to blame. Either way, the future wasn't looking bright for them. If I couldn't stop Fran from killing this guy, then things would get complicated.

Looks like I'll just have to use telekinesis and—

"Excuse me."

"Hrm? Colbert?"

"Sorry, mister. But this girl's under the employ of Count Bayreeds. If you want to recruit her, then you'll have to ask him first."

Oh yeah, I guess she is still under contract.

Formally speaking, Fran was working for House Bayreeds, and the baron backed off as soon as he heard the count's name.

"What? Bayreeds...?"

"That's right."

"H-hah! I shall take personal responsibility for my actions!"

"So, you're going to ignore the good count and recruit her anyway?" Colbert asked.

"Urgh..."

The baron and his guards were visibly distressed. He was insignificant compared to the count—one of the pillars of the kingdom. There would be no contest here.

The baron looked at his two guards and they shook

their heads, faces pale. They should've been able to gauge how strong Colbert was. They probably recognized him the moment he stepped in.

"F-fine! A beastman is not worthy of my house anyway!"

And then the baron escaped in one piece.

"Looks like I came just in time," said Colbert.

Fran paused. "Hm."

"What? You don't look too happy."

"He got away."

"Come on, Fran. You're getting famous now. You'll be seeing more and more of his kind soon enough. Are you just gonna beat all of them up?"

"No. I'll cut them down."

"No, dumbass! Then they'll stick a bounty on your head! Just do your best to ignore them."

That's right, Colbert. Tell her what's good for her. I'll even overlook the fact that you called her a dumbass!

"Which reminds me," he said. "I have business with you too. Message from the count. He says, 'Sorry about the mess we're in. Consider our contract concluded. However, if you need to refuse other nobles, feel free to use the name of House Bayreeds.'"

That was nice of him. Nobles would be sure to pester Fran as long as she was in the capital, but Count Bayreeds had enough influence to deflect their invitations.

"I'll be on my way, then," said Colbert. "I've still got work to do myself."

"Hm."

"And...I'm sorry about the Master of Curry."

"?"

Oh, right. Colbert still thought I died during the battle with Velmeria.

"We lost a great man today..."

Fran, Colbert thinks I'm dead. Can you please tell him that I'm alive?

"Teacher's not dead," Fran said.

Colbert looked perplexed for a moment, and then nodded sagely.

"Yeah," he said. "You're right."

"Hm."

"As long as someone carries on his legacy, that man will never die."

And so, the misunderstanding persisted, but Colbert left before Fran could clarify what she meant.

"Colbert was acting funny."

We'll have to set the record straight the next time we see him.

"Hm."

With Colbert gone, we could finally enter the guild.

"Huh?"

But just as Fran was about to go in, she backed away—just in time to avoid something hurtling out of the door. Or rather, *someone.* He tumbled until he lay flat on the road.

"Uhh…"

He was an adventurer. C-Rank. Decently strong. He was unconscious, but not dead.

"G-Gareth! Are you all right?!"

A small, pudgy man chased after Gareth. Probably a friend and fellow adventurer. What was going on here?

"Murderous intent?" Fran muttered.

Fran's sharpened senses told her that, whatever was inside the guild, it was dangerous. She readied herself.

An attack by the marquis' remnants?

"Hm. I'm going in!"

Be careful!"

Fran reached carefully for the door.

"How dare you waste our precious time with this nonsense during an emergency like this! And while I'm hurting over the destruction of the theater! You're lucky I didn't kill you!"

It was Erianthe. She shouted ferociously at the unconscious man, looking quite demonic with her disheveled purple hair.

"What happened?" Fran asked.

"Fran? Sorry about that. I thought you were another one of those idiots."

"The ones that just got kicked out?"

"Yes. What a waste of time they are!"

"What happened?"

"Listen to this—"

Still simmering with anger, Erianthe quickly rattled off an explanation. From what I could gather, the short fat man was named Desla, and he was the guildmaster of a post town not far from the capital. He managed adventurers, as well as supplies, and was otherwise a hardworking guildmaster. But he also coveted Erianthe's position and was quite bitter that a woman had taken the spot. Whenever they met, he always disagreed with her, but this time he had gone too far. He blamed Erianthe for the current disaster, and tried to pressure her to resign. Not only that, but he also said that "women aren't fit to be guildmaster" and "I feel sorry for your members," among other things. He even brought a C-Rank adventurer along to intimidate her.

"Intimidate you?" Fran asked.

With a *C-Rank*? I mean Fran was a C-Rank, sure, but she was unusually powerful. The man Erianthe kicked out the door was a true C-Rank.

"They apparently thought that a former mercenary

couldn't handle herself," Erianthe shouted, making sure the two men could hear her. "Well, they got that wrong!"

"What should we do with them, guildmaster?" one of her men asked.

He approached carefully. In fact, *everyone* in the guild was walking on eggshells, trying to avoid Erianthe's wrath. It felt like the whole guild was holding its breath, but Erianthe waved her hand, dismissing her men. She had had her fill.

"Leave them be. We have no time for idiots who don't know how to behave themselves in an emergency. He acts like a big shot, but the other guildmasters hate his guts. Once I make a report about this, he'll get fired."

"Uh-huh."

Fran wasn't interested, but she nodded along anyway. But her eyes were locked on the guildmaster's hair.

"Why does your hair change color?" Fran asked.

Erianthe's hair was usually blue, but it was purple in the battle earlier, and it was purple again now.

"Oh, this? It's my combat color. You see it in insectoids sometimes. I guess I have the genes for it. It changes color when I'm feeling aggressive."

Not all insectoids and their halflings had this feature, but then again, their characteristics varied wildly—even amongst halflings of the same type.

"Some people change during battle," said Erianthe. "Others stay the same."

"Like the mercenaries at the plaza?"

"That's right."

Robin the lobster and Hobbes the grasshopper both changed in a fight. Outside of battle, they looked mostly ordinary. Meanwhile, Effie the mayfly and Shingen the clam kept their insectoid features all the time, while Ann the bull ant always looked quite human.

"Are they your friends?" Fran asked.

"Yes... Old friends."

I was sure they were the remnants of Erianthe's old unit, and I really wanted to hear the story, but I knew we couldn't press the issue.

Fran, you should tell her the truth about my supposed death.

"Erianthe, Teacher's—"

But before Fran could finish, a man shouted from somewhere inside the guild.

"Guildmaster, a messenger eagle just came in!"

He came down from the second floor with a letter in hand. He'd crumpled it up a little in his excitement.

"Where's it from?"

"Northern border. From the guildmaster of Alessa!"

"Is it something to do with Raydoss?!"

"Yes! A Raydoss scout unit crossed the border and clashed with Alessan knights."

Now of all times?! Was Fanatix connected with Raydoss too?

"Go on!" said Erianthe. "What happened next?"

"R-right. With the help of B-Rank adventurer named Jean du Vix, the Raydoss threat was eliminated!"

Elated cheers erupted from the guild. Applause thundered through the halls. Everyone immediately accepted that the report was true. With the help of the knights, a single B-Rank had managed to turn the tide of battle and destroyed a squadron of Raydoss soldiers. This was no mere feat.

Erianthe sighed. "That's Slaughterfield for you!"

I had almost forgotten about Jean's grotesque nickname.

"Jean's so strong."

"That man's as good as an A-Rank when it comes to dealing with armies. He could take down an actual strike team by himself. Scouts should be no problem."

Apparently, the necromancer with the creepy laugh had saved Granzell. Jean's necromancy definitely gave him the upper hand on the battlefield. His undead soldiers probably overwhelmed the Raydossian scouts.

"I'll take this message to the king! Spread this news wherever you can! We could all use a lift right now!"

Erianthe's subordinates followed her orders and left the guild to spread the word.

I guess the clarification of my death will have to wait...

SIDE: VELMERIA

"Ah..."

I can't move. Where am I?

"Velmeria, are you awake?"

Frederick?

"Uhh... Aahh..."

I can't talk. I can't even lift a finger. What happened to me?

"Urslars, Velmeria has come to."

"Really? That's great. Glad to have you back."

This ogrekin...! The enemy!

"Urgh...!"

What's happening to my body? Who is this ogrekin? And why did I think he was an enemy? I've never even met him before...have I?

"I'm sorry I couldn't protect you, Velmeria."

"?"

"I failed as your guardian!"

What are you saying?

Frederick clasped his hands around mine. I could feel his tears running down my fingers.

"Slow down, Frederick," the ogrekin consoled him. "Her body must be exhausted from using all those skills at once. She might not even have her memories straight yet."

"Y-you're right. I'm sorry..."

"Excuse me, miss."

The ogrekin pressed his hand on my forehead. It was cold. Nice. I must've had a fever.

Frederick had called the ogrekin Urslars. Was it *that* Urslars? He *was* an ogrekin...

"The worst is over," said the ogrekin. "She needs to rest for now."

"I see... Go back to sleep, Velmeria. There's no need to force yourself."

"Uhh..."

What happened to me? I couldn't even nod. I had an argument with father and then...we were attacked! A man with a sword in his back took me away and...

And then what?

They put a broken sword in my hand—

"Ah!"

My head! It's like splitting apart!

"Miss! What happened?!"

"Velmeria!"

Aaaaaaaah! I remember! Me! Fanatix! The capital! I destroyed everything with my own hands!

"Aaah...!"

"I think her memories are coming back! Miss! What happened was not your fault! You are not to blame!"

"Velmeria, stop thinking about it!"

I killed them all! Father's men! Adventurers! All of them!

"She's losing it," said the ogrekin. "Shinryu Form is going activate again!"

"Wh-what should we do?!"

"Dammit! Frederick, she needs to calm down. Put her to sleep!"

"Forgive me, Velmeria!"

How could I have done that?! I...! I...!

I...

"Is she out?"

"No, I just gave her a sedative. Anesthetics won't work on her in her current aggravated state."

"We'll have to make sure she doesn't think about the capital for a while."

"I'm sorry."

"Hey, don't worry about it," said the ogrekin. "We'll get through this. I'll pacify her myself if it comes to it."

"To think that she still has Shinryu Form..."

People were talking around me...

It felt like something terrible had happened, but I couldn't remember what.

Whatever it is, I don't want *to remember...*

The voices were comforting. As I listened to them, all my worries melted away.

So tired... I can sleep now...right?

I'm sorry.

But why am I apologizing?

I can't stay awake any longer. Good night...

Reincarnated as a sword

6
King Granzell

TWO DAYS PASSED. Peace had yet to return to the capital, but at least the fighting had stopped, and the marquis' men were no more. But shortages of food, shelter, and medicine continued. Tensions were mounting. If it kept going like this, a riot might break out.

The main problem was shelter. Tents had been set up for the people who lost their homes, but there weren't enough to go around. At least some of the problem was because the nobles were claiming whole tents for themselves. So, somewhere that could have housed twenty people now only housed two or three. And there were enough nobles doing this to cause an issue.

At first, I thought they should just stick the nobles in together with the commoners, but that would be problematic. For starters, sharing a living space with some stuck-up nobles would be torturous. It would be more comfortable to sleep on the streets with a blanket. Nobles also had bigger egos than adventurers, so rank became a problem. A count would not stand to share living quarters with a baron. Even during an emergency, they had to save face.

Eventually, the commoners who shared tents with a noble moved to stay with their friends and relatives, but the bickering continued. Nobles regularly complained that it was an insult to have to live in such conditions. Some of them even commandeered the houses of commoners. Fights broke out, and the chasm between the lives of the rich and the poor grew deeper.

To make things worse, strong winds stirred up the ruins of the noble district, causing dust storms. Fran set up wind barriers around the shelters, and people were very grateful for it. Some nobles ordered her to put up barriers around their tents, but of course she refused anyone who didn't ask with common courtesy.

Still, aid had started coming in from neighboring cities, including food and security personnel. More helping hands were expected to come from all over the kingdom. Meanwhile, adventurers and soldiers were clearing up the rubble while the knights kept the peace.

The royal family was safe and had been moved to a secure location. Apparently, they were staying at a noble villa in the residential area. I had no idea what the king was like. The only impression I had of kings came from comic books. Specifically, the ones that said things like "a king must protect his men!" as the palace crumbled around him. But a *real* king would have to be as strong as the Beast King to do that. For normal rulers, it was more prudent to get somewhere safe. After all, a king could do more good for his kingdom and citizens by guiding them through the reconstruction efforts than by stubbornly dying in his castle.

"Sorry to keep you."

"It's okay."

"Indeed."

We were visiting Count Bayreeds, who was staying in one of the knight's stations after his manor was destroyed. I thought we would have left by now, but the capital needed all the help it could get.

"Why did you call us?"

"Well, I wanted to thank you for telling me the details of the incident. You were a great help. Both of you."

The count already knew that Velmeria was alive and in Urslars' care. As much as he grieved her loss, he was thankful that she was still alive. Bayreeds had let Velmeria go, but Fredrick, the Drakefiend Halfling, had gone with her. He disappeared as soon as the conversation was over, despite the injuries Fanatix had inflicted upon him. I suppose he was more loyal to Velmeria than to the count.

"Where should I start?" Bayreed mused. "I think you'll be happy to know that the state won't be pressing charges against Garrus. However, he will be assigned guards to monitor him for the time being."

"Really?"

"Yes. He was acquitted of all crimes once it was clear that he was being manipulated. And besides, it would be foolish to punish him, given the current chaos."

"What do you mean?"

"His Highness prioritizes the kingdom's well-being above everything else. The country has already suffered enough damage to its national power and pride. That situation must not be allowed to get any worse."

The threat of Raydoss loomed large from the north, and the notion of an ever-loyal class of nobles was shattered by this incident. But how was Garrus tied to national interest?

"Even before this, Garrus was the closest thing we had to a Godsmith. Now, he's actually *touched* a Godsword. It is better to turn the other cheek to his involvement and let him work for the kingdom instead of punishing him. Besides, there's also the matter of the Adventurer's Guild."

KING GRANZELL

"...?"

Fran tilted her head, but Forlund knew what the count meant.

"Favors."

"That's right. A lot of adventurers owe Garrus their livelihoods. Imagine the outrage if we charged him with crimes."

Garrus traveled across Granzell, selling quality equipment to adventurers for cheap. We were among such adventurers when we met him in Alessa. Fran had just started out, but even then, he provided her with excellent armor. There were probably countless adventurers like her who owed their first gear set to him.

"This country is home to a large population of adventurers. There was that large influx after Raydoss expelled them from their kingdom. Afterward, we made policies which gave preferential treatment to adventurers."

"Uh-huh."

"I can see you don't understand, Fran. We have five A-Ranks, and over ten former A-Ranks. Granzell is the only one with that many adventurers among the people. Of course, there are fewer of them now, but even so..."

We only really knew about Granzell and the Beastman Nation. The latter had a former adventurer for a king, but these two were the exception rather than the rule.

Adventurers were given tax breaks here, which made their lives easier.

"That isn't without its problems. Granzellian knights and soldiers are weaker as a result, but that's a subject for another time."

With more adventurers around, fewer knights and soldiers were needed for monster hunts, making it difficult for them to level up. Knights were always intended to deal with people rather than beasts, and so the knights of Granzell specialized in civilian peacekeeping.

"In any case, adventurers have a lot of power here, and the state will need to call upon that power in the future. Adventurers will become pivotal in the coming years."

The last thing the state wanted was to annoy them. Garrus had been saved by his deeds.

Meanwhile, Count Bayreeds had also escaped severe punishment. He *was* relieved of his office as Knight Commander, but all he had to do was pay a pittance in damages—or otherwise work them off.

"I was prepared to give up my lands and be confined in my own home..."

The count had failed to prevent a rebellion and thereby allowed most of the capital to be destroyed. Furthermore, his own daughter was one of the prime agents in the destruction. As Knight Commander, he was more than ready to take responsibility for what had happened, but the king had other plans. Instead of charging the count with negligence, he simply shifted the blame to Marquis Aschtner for secretly housing Fanatix. The king must have felt it more prudent to enlist Count Bayreeds' help in reconstructing of the capital. And, after all the destruction and loss of life it had suffered, the capital would need all the help it could get. Ultimately, the king was quite measured in his judgment of the situation.

Did that mean Velmeria was off the hook?

"The casualties and destruction my daughter caused were far too great. She attacked the palace—even if she *was* being manipulated. Besides, there are too many witnesses who saw what she did."

Compared to the self-destructing soldiers, the damage Velmeria caused was on another level. Granting her amnesty would set a bad precedent.

"For now, the king has assumed direct control of Aschtner's lands, as well as the lands of his accomplices. They will be redistributed at a later date."

Probably to the nobles who lost the most in this disaster.

"One last thing. The two of you have been summoned to have an audience with the king. You are to go to the mansion where he is staying today."

Wait? The king? As in the ruler of Granzell?

"Why?"

Bayreeds sighed. "You have no idea how much influence you wield, do you?"

Forlund was a known hero, sure, but Fran was also getting famous among the people that she healed, and placing in Ulmutt's fighting tournament only added to her fame. Now, as far as the capital was concerned, she was as famous as Forlund—we just didn't know it yet. After all, we'd spent the last two days away from other people, clearing away rubble. And we had moved through the city with teleportation and Air Hop, so Fran was too fast for ordinary people to spot.

"Forlund tells me your teacher was a great help in the battle."

Rumors that Fran's master—me—sacrificed himself for the sake of the capital were beginning to spread—probably because of Erianthe and Colbert. And we'd been so busy that we hadn't had time to clarify the situation. Still, I wasn't expecting that to reach the king!

"His Highness would like to show his appreciation to the heroes of the capital. I suppose he wants to make it clear to the citizens that he is on your side."

Not politics again!

Fran felt the same way and let it show, but Bayreeds just gave her a wry laugh.

"Not to worry. His Highness doesn't expect perfect manners from adventurers. I doubt the guild would stand idly by if he did, and he knows that better than anyone. He only wishes to chat with you."

It wasn't like we could turn down the king's invitation. If we'd heard about it earlier, we might have been able to flee the capital, but it was too late for that now. Annoying as it was, we had no choice but to accept.

A few hours later, Fran, Forlund, and I found ourselves inside a mansion. It wasn't very big, but it was clean and well-furnished. As the chamberlain led us down a hallway, I could feel a strange tension in the air. This was where the king was staying, and where he was tending to all the matters of the state.

Since the capital was in a state of emergency, Fran and Forlund were told to forego the formalwear, and as usual, they'd taken the suggestion at face value. Still, no weapons were allowed in, so I morphed myself into a bracelet for the time being. They would barely even notice me. At least all of this would be over quickly—after all, it was too early for dinner and too late for teatime.

The mansion was filled with knights, which was to be expected right after a rebellion. The tension I felt was their collective Intimidation. They knew the mansion was not easy to defend, so even guests like Fran and

Forlund got the brunt of it. But the two of them weren't offended—they knew the weight of the knights' responsibility. In fact, they were so relaxed that it didn't feel like they were going to meet the king at all.

Fran, you have to be polite when speaking with the king, all right? I'm serious now.

"Hm."

Actually, try not to say anything out of turn.

"Hm."

Nope! I'm still worried! Will she be okay? She's going to have an audience with the king here. The KING!

Are you sure you'll be okay? If you don't know what to say, just don't say anything. You don't wanna be rude.

"I know."

Forlund looked like a veteran, but Fran was still a beginner. And if she wasn't worried, then I was *certainly* worried for her. Of course, she had met the Beast King before, but he was hardly the measuring stick for how royalty behaved.

Forlund, please back her up if anything goes wrong! I'm begging you!

Very well, replied Forlund. *But you have nothing to worry about. The king of these lands is not so shallow as to be upset by awkward manners. As long as people aren't rude to him on purpose, it will be fine.*

You say that, but...

We were talking about Fran here—a girl who didn't show nobles even a shred of respect. I mean, most of them didn't deserve respect in the first place, but politeness was an issue in this case.

I'm ready to flee the country if things go south...

"I'll be fine," said Fran. "Trust me."

"You worry too much," Forlund agreed.

How can you two be so calm...?

Despite my anxieties, it was soon time for our audience. The chamberlain leading Fran and Forlund stopped outside a large door. It was a dining room, ordinarily used for entertaining guests, and large enough to serve as a provisional audience room.

"The king is beyond these doors. Pray, conduct yourselves properly."

"Hm."

"Sir."

The old chamberlain stared at them. "Very well."

He was probably thinking, "I wonder if these two will be all right?" I felt the same way.

Just like we practiced, Fran.

Hm.

The door opened from the inside, revealing a simple audience room. It was probably modified after the king decided to move in. A red carpet came out of nowhere, extending from the door all the way to the throne. The throne was much simpler than the one we saw in the Beastman Nation, but it was still extravagant. A middle-aged man in lavish clothing sat upon it, and if I was being honest, he looked a bit out of place.

He wore a thick red robe which restricted his movement and made him look like a bishop. His feet were adorned with sparkling sandals, and a small crown adorned his head. I assumed it must've been one made for everyday use. The sight was quite breathtaking.

The man was around fifty years old, and while his hairline was beginning to recede, his body was quite well-built. Not as much as a warrior, but enough to showcase his discipline. He wasn't a tyrant with a beer belly, that was sure. This king was nothing like the powerful rulers we had gotten acquainted with in our travels. Although to be fair, our points of comparison were the S-Rank Beast King and the Phyllius royals who possessed their own Godsword.

Knights and nobles stood on either side of him, and I could tell that half the nobles were looking down on Fran. Still, the other half happily welcomed her and Forlund both. In fact, most of the better-dressed nobles seemed to feel that way. They recognized the importance of adventurers in Granzell. The knights, on the other hand, remained as stone-faced as ever. The strongest among them stood closest to the king, and he was a very strong man, indeed.

His skin was white as snow and his hair was fine as silver. He was only around 180 centimeters tall, but the pressure and mana he gave off amplified his presence. I once heard that bodyguards looked intimidating to deter potential assailants, but this man was on another level. He declared his strength to everyone who approached the king so they would think twice before doing anything funny. On the flip side, anyone who couldn't sense his strength wasn't worth his attention.

He has no blind spots...

He was probably around A-Rank in strength, but unfortunately, I couldn't use Identify. After all, we were in the presence of royalty. This man was the king's royal guard, and perfectly positioned to attack Fran and Forlund if he had to.

"Go forth," the chamberlain said.

Fran and Forlund stepped forward and bent at the knee. *Good, just as we practiced.* In fact, Fran's etiquette was so proper that it shocked the nobles. They weren't expecting this little adventurer to be so well versed in court etiquette. In the end, Baron Allsand was good for something. His Court Etiquette Skill was top-notch.

"We are extremely honored to have been granted audience with Your Highness," Forlund said.

Fran remained quiet and kept her head down. The chamberlain told them that that was good enough. Somehow, things were working out.

"Arise," the king said.

"Your Highness," the two of them said, raising their heads.

So far, so good.

"You have done a great service to the kingdom."

They nodded. "Your Highness."

Everything was going according to plan. The audience continued just as formally, until the king gave them his compliments and drew things to a close. There wasn't any small talk at all. What a letdown.

I was expecting him to talk about the future of Granzell or something.

Hm.

No court ranks offered. No awards. Nothing.

We had talked to Erianthe before we left, and she had told us to be careful about refusing a court rank. That could come back to bite us in the ass later. Instead, if Fran awarded a rank, Erianthe advised her to show the Golden Beast Fang Award she'd received in the Beastman Nation.

That award had come in handy *outside* the audience room too. After that idiot noble had tried to recruit Fran the other day, there were many more who wanted to associate themselves with the Black Cat Saint. Didn't they have anything better to do while the capital was in crisis? Apparently not. They hadn't been asked to help with the important task of reconstruction, and judging by how stupid they were when they approached Fran, that was probably for the best.

But there were *so* many of them, and some even refused to back down after we namedropped the count. We asked Erianthe what to do, and the Golden Beast Fang was her solution. The award was much more powerful than we initially thought. When Fran showed it to her, Erianthe literally jumped.

Not that foreign awards carried much weight in Granzell, but it *did* show that Fran was connected to the Beastman Nation in a significant way. She was a beastman after all, so she could pass as a native of that land. And, since the Beastman Nation Granzell's ally, Erianthe supposed that showing the award would deter any forceful invitations.

I didn't want people thinking that Fran was in the pocket of the Beastman Nation, but she *was* comfortable there, and it was much better than having a court rank forced upon her. Maybe the Beast King knew that it would help her when he gave her the award. Anyway, I was worrying too much—so much that I felt like I'd lost a few pounds, just from worrying. Had my blade gotten thinner?

Anyway, I needn't have worried—the audience ended quietly and without interruption.

"You two."

But just when I was breathing a sigh of relief, the chamberlain stopped us on our way out of the mansion. That didn't bode well, and the next words out of his mouth were the very ones that I didn't want to hear.

"The king is waiting for you in another room. Right this way."

The chamberlain didn't wait for Fran and Forlund's response before leading the way. I guess he thought it was impossible for them to disobey him.

Fran, remember to be polite.

"Hm? Sure."

Had she forgotten? If she had, then I'm glad I reminded her!

We walked through the mansion for a few minutes before reaching the room where the person I didn't want to meet was waiting for us.

The chamberlain motioned to a couch. "Please."

"Sir."

"Hm."

Fran and Forlund sat on the sofa, and quite a comfortable sofa it was. I guess that was one of the perks of living in a mansion. We were now in a snug little drawing room which was smaller than the audience room from earlier, but that only made me even *more* nervous. The king was closer to us now—his sofa was only three meters away from ours.

"Relax," he said. "This is not an official meeting."

So he says, but no one's going to take that at face value.

"Hm."

No one except Fran, that is! No, we're still okay. She's only relaxed her shoulders. She can still recover!

Fran, don't let your guard down!

Hm?

Uh, just sit straight for as long as you're here!

All right.

That was close. But at least my girl could sit as straight as a board if she wanted to!

Now if only Sir Silver Hair would stop glaring at her. You're going to make her think you want to fight! Things won't end well if the two of you clash!

As I was freaking out, the king started speaking.

"I am Wisolla Bredd Granzell."

This was certainly the same man we met in the audience room, but now he seemed way too relaxed for comfort. I scanned the room and only detected the king, two knights, and the chamberlain. Usually, they would have guards hiding behind the walls, but not this time.

Fran tilted her head, and the king caught her eye.

"What is it, child?"

"Why...does Your Highness not have guards?"

"Ah. I told my knights that they would not be necessary. They would only be a hindrance if the two of you were to attack." The king looked intently at Fran. "You don't seem very strong by my count, but..."

Apparently, the king had an Identification Skill of some kind. But Fake Identify meant that she only appeared to be an average adventurer. However, it didn't fool the silver-haired knight next to him.

"She is at least as strong as I," he said.

"And I have no reason to doubt Luga's words. Allow me to introduce you. This is the Captain of the Royal Guard, the King's Knight, Luga Moufle."

"Pleased to make your acquaintance."

Luga Moufle, the silver-haired knight, greeted Fran and Forlund without taking his eyes off of them. This man was meticulous to a tee.

"He is among the few powerful warriors of my kingdom. I trust you will see each other quite frequently."

The king emphasized the words *my kingdom*. He really

wanted Fran and Forlund on Granzell's side. But King Granzell was quite different from the Beast King. While Rigdith was an intimidating warrior, the man in front of us was more politician than fighter. Even so, he did not lack the dignity of a king. Although he told us to be at ease earlier, he made it perfectly clear that he was peerless in this room. He had the quiet grandeur of the true elite. I appreciated the fact that he wasn't an idiot, but that meant we shouldn't let our guard down.

"Let us get down to business. We do not have time to waste."

The king glanced at the chamberlain, and the old man immediately took out two small boxes, about thirty centimeters in length. He set them before Fran and Forlund. Inside was a medal decorated with jewels.

"These belong to the highest rank of the nobility."

Well, that came out of nowhere. We couldn't be roundabout in rejecting this either. Was there an ulterior motive behind this gift? Or was it granted from the goodness of the king's heart? I couldn't tell by looking at him.

Teacher? Fran asked.

Hang on. Forlund, what should we do?

Telepathy was very useful at times like this.

I see, said Forlund. *Fran doesn't wish to accept the title?*

Of course not.

Forlund nodded. *Very well. Let me handle this.*

He was so reliable!

"As much as we appreciate Your Highness' offer..."

Forlund looked the king in the eye and shook his head.

"You would refuse?" the king asked.

"As I did the last time. The same goes for her."

"Hm. I refuse."

Fran! Wording!

Royal Etiquette helped with Fran's mannerisms, but not her vocabulary. I told her to rephrase.

"I'm sorry. I would like to continue being an adventurer."

"Even though *I* am granting this to you?"

The king furled his eyebrows with disdain, and Luga Moufle increased his Intimidation. Was he getting ready to throw down?

Pressure filled the room. This was when the weak and the flatterers would fold. Even I was getting queasy in my nonexistent stomach.

"Most unfortunate," Forlund bowed.

"I apologize," Fran said, following his cue.

The two of them treated Luga's pressure like a faint breeze, but to me, the silence was stifling. King Granzell frowned.

"It is as you said, Luga," he scoffed, sinking into his sofa.

"They are adventurers, Your Highness."

"I was right to do this away from the lower nobles. Imagine the noise they would make."

At least they both seemed to expect it.

"They have no idea how much they owe to adventurers," he sighed. "Even the greatest among them are beginning to forget…"

The king planned to give Fran and Forlund their ranks away from the nobles so that the nobles wouldn't hate them. Was their disdain also an act? And yet it remained there.

"This isn't the first time I've offered this gift to Hundred Blade Forlund, so I was expecting his refusal. But why do you refuse, Black Lightning Princess? I know your kind hates managing land, but you would not need to. At the highest rank of nobility, you would be like a count without a territory. I thought you would appreciate this gift."

It was a court rank for adventurers. In exchange for the yearly noble taxes, the adventurer swore fealty to the kingdom. Since they were no longer considered adventurers, they could participate in wars. In exchange, the adventurer would gain honor, as well as the backing of the kingdom.

"Why is it that you will not accept?"

Forlund answered the king's question simply. "Freedom."

"I am afraid that I am unfamiliar with that word," the king scoffed. "Aren't you the least bit interested in power and money? What about you, child?"

"I don't...have no particular interest in such things."

"'In such things'...! You adventurers are always...! But never mind. You may leave."

Did we upset the king? At least Luga didn't show any signs of attacking us. Maybe it was because he expected us to refuse in the first place. I guess he wanted us to know that he was still displeased regardless.

"Forget everything that happened here," the king said as we were leaving. "I shall forget as well."

His anger was still there, but he didn't want to make enemies of us. That's why he wanted us to forget his less-than-kingly conduct.

Phew. Well, at least that worked out somehow. Honestly, I was planning to leave the country.

As I said yesterday, said Forlund. *The king places the good of the kingdom above everything else. He is not so foolish as to make enemies of us. Of course, if he thought it was better for the kingdom if he were to save face, he would've attacked us on the spot.*

King Granzell wasn't one to give in to his emotions, but he was still intimidating. A different kind of intimidating from the Beast King perhaps, but he still put pressure on us.

I'm just glad we made it out in one piece.

With the audience over, we made our way back to the Adventurer's Guild. Erianthe had asked to see us. When we got there, the place was packed with adventurers. It wasn't quite as busy as a Japanese train during rush hour—maybe more like a children's schoolyard during recess. With all the aid coming from nearby towns, the adventurer population had at least doubled. There weren't enough beds to go around, and many had taken to sleeping on the floor in the guild hall.

Fran was already famous among the local adventurers, but some out-of-towners would want to mess with her. The low-rank adventurers were mostly in charge of clearing the rubble, and while some went about the work with magic and skills, 80 percent used good old-fashioned manpower. That meant that most of them weren't strong enough to sense Fran's strength.

Many of these adventurers probably dreamed of coming to the capital and working on exciting quests. But when they got here, they were greeted by mountains of rubble, and the only work awaiting them was the hard labor of reconstruction. Adventurers weren't saints, and many were all too eager to vent their frustrations on a little girl, but no such adventurer came at Fran today. Maybe they heard about what happened to the people who came at her yesterday and the day before.

To be clear, we healed them back up afterwards. After all, the capital couldn't afford to lose any manpower. But we also told them that worse things would happen if they didn't take their job seriously. Right now, they were probably working up a good, productive sweat. And apparently, the story had spread to the newcomers, because no one bothered Fran today. In fact, they looked terrified when they saw her.

"Stellia."

"Come on up!"

"Okay."

The high-rank lines were temporarily closed to make room for more low-rank adventurers, and Stellia was busier than ever. It had to be tough work keeping all these adventurers in line, but she was managing it well. Usually, adventurers flocked to the prettiest receptionist, leaving Stellia's line deserted, but today...

"Hey! There's a line here over here! Stop complaining and shut the hell up!"

Stellia was using Intimidate to get the newcomers in line. They looked pale by the time they were organized, and I wished them the best of luck.

We left the ruckus of the first floor and arrived at Erianthe's office.

"So much work... Never-ending work..."

Oof.

"Paper mountain."

All the paperwork had somehow increased since the last time we saw it, and Erianthe sat in the center of it all, looking haggard and ghastly.

"Erianthe?"

"Oh," she groaned. "You're here... Hang on."

"Hm."

Over the next five minutes, Erianthe had calmed herself down with a cup of tea and gave Fran some documents.

"What's this?" Fran asked.

"Your appointment letter. You're getting promoted to B-Rank."

"Hm? I'm promoted? Why?"

That came out of nowhere. Fran hadn't done enough to even be eligible.

Erianthe sighed. "Do you know how much you've accomplished in this incident? You defeated the monster that annihilated Zefield and his party, you healed hundreds of people, moved mountains of rubble...and gods only know all the other things you did."

Now that she mentioned it, Fran *had* done a whole a lot. Aside from Urslars and Forlund, no one else had contributed more during this incident.

"I know you don't like the hassle of promotion, but the things that were holding you back are no longer applicable. Not after what happened in the capital."

"What do you mean?"

"Your combat rating was never really a problem. You're as good as an A-Rank, really. But now we finally have evidence of that."

Erianthe had seen the battle against the marquis, and if she wasn't a good judge of combat strength, no one was. Fran had proven herself in actual combat instead of a simulated duel.

"Moving on to your accomplishments, you've made a name for yourself in the capital, and have been awarded a medal from the Beastman Nation. So, you have more than enough."

Certainly enough to make B-Rank.

"As for your attitude toward nobility, your audience with the king has proven that you have at least a base level of manners and courtesy."

So that was it.

B-Ranks had more dealings with nobility, and the guild had been worried about how Fran would treat them. They weren't off-base to be worried, but she'd proved them wrong during her audience with the pinnacle of nobility—the king.

"A noble acquaintance of mine said your etiquette was perfect. In fact, you behaved better than most lower-ranking nobles. It shocked them."

Her friend must have been one of the nobles standing around the king.

"And I hear you refused the gift of a court rank?" Erianthe asked.

"Hm. But he was mad about it."

"Oh, the king isn't mad at you. Maybe he had to act that way so adventurers wouldn't make light of him." Erianthe paused. "Anyway. While the king isn't to be trifled with, he doesn't act on his emotions. And he would never do something stupid like make an enemy of you. You can count on that."

So the king *was* acting. He must have wanted to show that he wasn't to be refused lightly. But at the same time, he still wanted Fran and Forlund to associate with him. That's why he asked them to forget his small outburst—which they had caused—to make them feel like they owed him. And so, he showed magnanimity and mercy to the adventurers who had so brazenly refused him. At least, that was how it looked like to anyone who didn't know better.

This way, if the king issued us a quest in the future, he could say, "You refused my honors before, so surely you will not refuse this quest?"

I mean, he still let a coup happen right under his nose, but at the same time, he really was the king of a great kingdom.

And King Granzell was up against Fanatix, after all. A Godsword that was nigh impossible to detect.

"He wouldn't try anything funny," said Erianthe. "Not when you have an award from the Beastman Nation. Granzell's relations with them will be pivotal in the near future. That's also why Count Bayreeds received a lighter punishment."

"Really?"

"Yes. Their relationship is quite famous. Rumor has it Bayreeds was removed from his position so that he could serve as envoy to the Beastman Nation."

Going easy on Bayreeds and assigning him as envoy would only strengthen Granzell's relationship with the Beastman Nation.

"Your award had a great effect on your promotion too," said Erianthe. "The guild was concerned that you were just a child who walloped nobility. But now they know that you have a powerful supporter."

Strong fighter, knew how to handle herself around nobility, had a powerful supporter. It was clear that there was no reason as to why Fran shouldn't be made B-Rank.

"Honestly, the other guildmasters have asked me to promote you no matter what, and the guild's integrity would come into question if we didn't. So congratulations, you're promoted!"

Erianthe made it sound like that was the end of it, but I saw the worry in her eyes. Fran still had the right to refuse. Moreover, she still had *reason* to refuse. After all, it would mean we didn't have to deal with so many pesky nobles. Even with Fran's sponsor, some nobles just wouldn't leave her alone.

What now, Fran?

Hm? I'm taking it.

Are you sure? It's going to further complicate things. Especially with idiot nobles and adventurers around.

I'll just kick their asses.

Right...

It was up to me to rein her in from now on, but I loved Fran's spirit. And so, we gratefully accepted the promotion.

A few days later, Fran was summoned to the Adventurer's Guild once more. People stared and whispered when she entered the hall, but none of them looked at her with scorn. Instead, they gazed at her with either respect or fear. The greenhorns were in awe of the youngest B-Rank in history, but the fear was from the people whose asses Fran had kicked—as well as those who'd witnessed the whooping.

Either way, I was glad that they kept their distance. I guess being promoted had its perks. In fact, fewer nobles were approaching Fran too, and rumors that she had the Beast King's backing were beginning to spread. Apparently, the king mentioned it at dinner one evening.

Of course, some nobles still approached her—mostly the ones who thought they were exceptional when they clearly weren't. If they were anything special, then they wouldn't be stuck with nothing to do right now. Still, a single Intimidate was enough to keep them away, so they didn't get in the way of our work much at all.

Even so, Fran had less and less to do over the past few days. The critically wounded were all healed, and the court doctors and mages were taking care of them now. Out of town adventurers were clearing the rubble, and knights were keeping public order.

But Fran still wanted to help. She asked Count Bayreeds if she should make temporary housing with Land spells, but he rejected her proposal. The outer walls were crawling with monsters so it was no place for anyone to live, and while the common district was densely populated, it had been spared most of the destruction. Even in the obliterated noble district, temporary housing wasn't viable. After all, it would have to be knocked down during reconstruction—driving up labor costs. Ultimately, tents were the more economical option.

To be honest, I was thinking about Earth's sensibilities when I made the proposal, but things were different in this world. For one thing, there were no prefab houses here, so any temporary accommodations would have to be destroyed sooner or later. So, as much as we wanted to help with the reconstruction, we wouldn't be staying much longer. Fran had healed the wounded and set up wind barriers to protect the people from sandstorms, but with those dangers pretty much past, she was left with nothing to do.

I guess that was why she was summoned back to the guild. However, this time it wasn't Erianthe who called her, but it was Forlund.

"I'm here," she said.

"Good."

The two were as wordless as ever. Forlund guided us down the hall, so I guess we weren't visiting Erianthe's office today.

"Here."

The room he led us to looked like a hotel room, so it was probably reserved for out-of-town adventurers who had business in the capital. There were times when adventurers couldn't use inns, either because of time or the nature of their work. When that happened, they stayed here.

"Garrus's room?" Fran asked.

"Yes."

Garrus was its current occupant. Although the state had determined not to sentence the blacksmith, he was still under the care of the Adventurer's Guild. Eiworth's knowledge of alchemy had helped keep him out of the state's hands, and the king wasn't going to do anything to upset the Adventurer's Guild. As for us, we decided to wait until Garrus woke up, so he could make the decision about what he wanted to do.

When Forlund entered the room, we found Eiworth, Erianthe, and Garrus were waiting for us. Garrus was sitting up and welcomed Fran as she came in.

"You're awake?" Fran asked.

"Yeah. Looks like I put you through a lot of trouble. Thanks. And sorry about everything."

He was still looking worse for wear, but at least he could talk now. I wondered if the last of the drugs had finally worn off.

"Are you okay now?" Fran asked.

Eiworth grinned. "Of course he is. After all, *I* was the one who treated him. I used only the finest spirit potions. Oh, don't worry about the cost. The guild has already agreed to pay me—they want this dwarf alive, after all. Besides, I received precious data during the process."

For a second, I almost thought that Eiworth was being modest by refusing payment. In fact, he was as opportunistic as ever, and treated Garrus' like any other experiment. Fortunately, it worked out, so we couldn't really complain.

"Also," said Eiworth. "I made a deal with the state."

"What kind of deal?"

"Can you believe that they complained after I used their weak mages?" he scoffed.

Eiworth had teamed up with the kingdom's mages and gave them a powerful potion. It boosted their strength and stamina, enabling them to fight without tiring, but the moment the potion wore off, they were struck with hellish soreness and insomnia.

"Of course they complained. They don't have any mages left to help with the reconstruction effort because of you."

"I eliminated the threat and prevented further damage," Eiworth protested.

"I know. That's why they aren't pressing charges, so long as you heal Garrus."

"Hmph. I know that."

"More importantly, we need to talk about what's going to happen to Garrus now. That's why we called you here today, Fran."

Fran was the one who issued Garrus' protection quest, after all. So, the guild had an obligation to her. Erianthe and Eiworth had already explained the situation to Garrus—even the parts the dwarf couldn't remember. Even so, he felt responsible for everything he'd done.

"What do you want to do, Garrus?" Fran asked.

Garrus groaned as he thought about it. His actions had contributed to the destruction of the capital, even if he *was* being manipulated against his will. He clenched his hands so hard that they trembled.

"I'll help you escape if you want," said Fran.

"The Thieves' Guild is also willing to assist you," Eiworth added.

"That goes for the Adventurer's Guild, as well," said Erianthe.

"As will I," Forlund said.

The guilds weren't optimistic about Garrus' fate. If the state got a hold of him, they might lock him up and force him to perform more research on Godswords. It was kind of them to offer, but Garrus shook his head.

"I'm staying. I don't know if I can atone for my sins, but I would like to help rebuild the city as best I can."

"Are you sure?"

"I am."

Garrus knew the implications of his decision, but still he decided he would turn himself over to the state. And, judging by the determined look on his face, nothing we could say would change his mind.

"I see," Fran muttered, disappointed.

"Sorry. After all you've done for me..."

"No, it's okay. As long as it's your choice."

"The guild will put the pressure on them, don't you worry!" said Erianthe.

"The Thieves' Guild won't sit idly by either," Eiworth added.

"And neither will I," said Forlund.

Garrus had a lot of supporters, so he would probably be okay. If nothing else, the state wouldn't detain him. If they did, they would have to face the wrath of several guilds and A-Ranks.

Garrus bowed his head. "Sorry about this."

In this heartfelt moment, who else could break the silence but Eiworth?

"Are we done talking about the tedious nonsense? We are? Excellent."

He took something out of his pocket—documents, like the ones from the other day—and started questioning Garrus. The questions were quite technical, and Eiworth referred back to his papers as they talked.

"I don't understand how this bit works—"

"Oh, that. You see—"

"Aha. So what you're saying is—"

"That would be here—"

Garrus couldn't ignore Eiworth—after all, he was treated him while he was sick. But Garrus didn't seem like he hated it either. In fact, the dwarf looked like he was enjoying himself.

Every time you get a bunch of researchers in a room, this is what happens!

The two of them carried on talking, ignorant of the exasperation in the room. Still, everyone was quite interested to hear more about the Fanatix replicas—especially Erianthe.

"And that about settles it."

"So the Fanatix replicas can no longer be produced?" she asked.

"They can't. The Mad Faith Sword was the primary ingredient, after all."

The first Fanatix replica was failed manatek, developed by the marquis' alchemists. It was designed to absorb mana from its user and their surroundings and unleash it in a jet. They got as far as making prototypes, but they were never as stable or powerful as they'd hoped.

However, Fanatix was interested in the idea, and decided to modify it to look like a sword. Next, it added pieces of itself to the production line so it could use the replicas as remote-controlled substitutes. Finally, the manatek became full replicas, with pieces of Fanatix's mind inside of them. They nullified mana because that's what the manatek was originally designed for, and were placed in the spine because that's how the manatek was equipped. Finally, they took the form of swords because Fanatix could only unleash its full potential in that shape.

"So now that the Sword of Mad Faith has been destroyed, the replicas can no longer be produced."

"But whether the state will buy that story or not is a different question."

"All this data cannot be fabricated out of thin air, and I'm sure they will discover more material at the marquis' properties soon enough. After that, even a fool will understand it."

Of course, the state would be interested in the Fanatix replicas. They might only be copies, but they were still replicas of a *Godsword*. However, if they lost control of the project, then the whole kingdom would be in danger, and King Granzell knew better than to follow that path. At the same time, the information the Thieves' Guild had gathered from servants at the marquis' house would show exactly how things played out once the marquis got his hands on Fanatix. Those thieves could be quite industrious.

Meanwhile, two things crossed my mind: Hummels' night raids, and why Velmeria was chosen as the target. First of all, Hummels and the others had attacked Fran because they were looking for a strong host. Once they spotted me, she became an even *more* enticing target since I was made of orichalcos. However, they came across Velmeria in the process. She was a drake from a unique bloodline that possessed a powerful skill called Shinryu Form. That's when Fanatix decided to kidnap her.

"That meant that Fanatix had to obtain the most powerful host it could before its plans could come to fruition."

"Plans?"

Eiworth chuckled. "The mad sword was quite mad, indeed."

He explained that the marquis discovered the Mad Faith Sword in one of his territories forty years ago. His expedition team were scouting the ruins of a hundred-year-old fort in order to repurpose it when they happened upon an underground compound overflowing with mana. The team presented the broken Godsword to the marquis, but since Fanatix was still alive, it took over. After that, the Godsword used all of the marquis' influence and power for its own ends.

"What? It was going to cooperate with Raydoss to occupy Phyllius?" Erianthe asked, bewildered.

"To be specific," said Eiworth. "It wanted Diablos."

"Same difference."

Fanatix wanted another Godsword so that it could mend itself. Of course, it needed Garrus to make more Fanatix replicas, but he was also needed to make repairs.

"So the Raydossian invasion that happened recently..."

"Was all part of the plan."

"I have a bad feeling about this," Erianthe muttered.

Her insectoid intuition must've been tingling, and that made me worry.

"We're not hiding the fact that Slaughterfield Jean is stationed at Alessa," she said. "In fact, we hope that the enemy will spread the word for us. After all, it will reduce their morale. But the fact that they're *still* attacking..."

"Means that the Godsword prepared them for that."

That didn't sound good. As strong as Jean was, he was up against a military state with a plan. There was a very real chance that he could be defeated.

"Wh-why is everyone so quiet?!" Erianthe asked.

"Well, it has nothing to do with me," Eiworth scoffed. The old man didn't care which way the kingdom went. But that wasn't the only reason why he was so calm. "Besides, the border town has Calamity to keep it safe."

"What?" said Erianthe. "That makes it even worse! If Klimt actually fights..."

Eiworth had mentioned Calamity Klimt before, but Erianthe seemed more afraid of Klimt than she was of the Raydossian forces.

"Why are you guys so worried about Klimt?" Fran asked.

Erianthe paused for a moment before laying down the hard facts.

"You're a B-Rank now, so I suppose I should tell you. Klimt is nicknamed The Calamity. He's a powerful sorcerer capable of raining down mass destruction on friend and foe alike."

So, his attacks covered a lot of ground, just like Urslars.

"He was mistakenly given this nickname fifty years ago by adventurers who didn't know any better. Now, most think that the nickname is warranted...but Klimt is the guild's trump card. Still, it's better if details of the incident never came to light."

"Mistakenly?" Fran asked.

"Yes. He actually saved a city and prevented mass destruction."

It happened a long time ago, in a small country north of Granzell. It was a lesser kingdom and a vassal state of Raydoss. Stuck between two powerful forces, the land was subject to the political whims of both of its powerful neighbors. War always threatened to break out, and its people were constantly on their toes, ready to fight for their lives. Eventually, the overwhelming pressure and a lack of funding forced them to cast their lot with Raydoss.

At least, that was until their king tried to break free. To achieve this, he set his eyes on Spirit Magic. It didn't cost much, so the king and invited druids to his country to develop it further. But Spirit Magic was exceptionally difficult and highly inconsistent when used by an untalented practitioner. Even if the same druid performed the same Spirit spell twice in a row, the results would change depending on their physical and mental condition and the whims of the spirit in question. Spirits didn't think like living things, so they were liable to carry out orders in unexpected ways.

Soldiers and adventurers considered Spirit Magic too difficult, too unstable, and too weak to be of much use. Unless you were an expert, it was also extremely inconsistent, and that was its Achilles' heel. Spirits went out of control far too often, and it took elves thousands of years of practice to make their spirits less volatile.

In the end, the small kingdom's experiments with Spirit Magic failed. The druids tried to summon a great spirit, but it quickly spiraled out of control. Miraculously, and unfortunately, they succeeded in summoning a greater spirit.

Spirits have a hierarchy of power: there are lower spirits, lesser spirits, intermediate spirits, great spirits, greater spirits, and king spirits. A greater spirit is as strong as an A-Threat monster—powerful enough to destroy a small country if it went berserk. The Greater Wind Spirit they summoned rampaged through the kingdom for five days, leveling over half the country, wounding and killing over fifty thousand people.

Finally, someone arrived to quell it—Klimt, the guildmaster of Alessa. He had stayed out of the experiments, but people who didn't know any better thought that Klimt summoned the spirit himself. To overcome it, he had to form a contract with the greater spirit, and after that, he seemed to have it under full control. That only contributed to the misunderstanding.

"In truth," said Erianthe. "The kingdom only narrowly avoided destruction. Klimt infiltrated enemy territory, and somehow managed to enter a contract with the spirit. As insane as it sounds to talk about, it actually worked. He really is a genius among druids."

"But Klimt got weaker as a result."

"How come?" Fran asked.

Shouldn't he have gotten stronger after having a contract with a powerful spirit? I thought that was how he became an S-Rank.

"His body is constantly straining to keep the greater spirit inside him in check. His mana output is much lower now, and his lifespan will be shorter as a result. The spirit even affected his physical body."

"He used to be able to control multiple great spirits in battle, but that's difficult for him now."

No wonder his physical stats were low when I Identified him back in Alessa. I thought that was just the standard for mages, but A-Ranks didn't usually have glaring weaknesses.

"But it's not like he can't fight," Erianthe said. "He can still use the greater spirit if push comes to shove."

Eiworth chuckled. "It's a Greater Wind Spirit. Powerful enough to blow everything away at the roots."

The Adventurer's Guild made Klimt the guildmaster of Alessa because he was Raydoss' mortal enemy. This was the country that expelled and executed adventurers and took over the Adventurer's Guild in its territory, after all. But Granzell was immediately south of Raydoss, and *they* provided adventurers with many benefits. And so Klimt was their trump card—assigned to protect their northern border.

"Still, a trump card is only played as a last resort. That's why Amanda and Jean are stationed in Alessa. We want to keep Klimt out of battle for as long as we can."

The day Klimt unleashed the greater spirit was the day the world faced a threat even more powerful than Amanda.

"When he enters the fray, his greater spirit will do tremendous damage to the surrounding area, and Klimt wouldn't be spared either. He used the spirit to fight a dragon once, and ended up in the afterlife for a short while. It's almost impossible to fully control something like that."

Eiworth chuckled. "I wonder who's more dangerous: Calamity or Friendly Fire?"

They both posed a threat to their own allies and were powerful enough to wipe out whole countries. It seemed that Klimt was far stronger than I gave him credit for.

Erianthe was afraid that he would summon the spirit and losing control of it. She talked a while longer about the defense of Alessa, but stopped when she noticed that Fran wanted to speak with Garrus. Eiworth complained, of course, since there was still so much to talk about, but Forlund dragged him away for us.

After that, Fran set up a soundproof barrier. You never knew if Eiworth was listening in.

"Thanks again," Garrus said. "I guess you found the scabbard I made?"

"Hm."

With that name and shape? I knew something was up.

"And I knew I could count on you to notice," said Garrus.

I'm glad things worked out, but you know there was a chance that we wouldn't come, right?

Garrus had no way of knowing that we would keep our promise. We might have been occupied at the time, or even died in our travels, but he only shook his head and smiled.

"Nah. I knew you'd come through. You look like the type to keep promises."

"Of course. I always keep my promises to my friends," said Fran.

"Ga ha ha! Friends, you say! Yeah, I guess we *are* friends!"

"Hm."

Garrus laughed, but it soon subsided, and his eyes filled up with sorrow. I couldn't help but feel sorry for him. I wondered what was wrong.

"Anyway. There's something I've been meaning to ask," he said.

"Hm?"

"Your equipment—is that my Black Cat set?"

Of course! Of course, he would wonder about Fran's gear. Her armor looked completely different from the day he made it.

I explained how that had happened: we fought a powerful enemy, and the armor was severely beat up. The Self Repair function was weakened, and a blacksmith we met offered to repair it for us.

"The blacksmith you happened to meet... Did they happen to be a Godsmith?" Garrus asked.

He noticed straight away. Garrus wasn't called the world's greatest blacksmith for nothing. He could appraise the craftmanship of something in an instant. He must've been sad because he was comparing Aristea's armor to his.

Uhh...

What now? Garrus' equipment had been modified without his consent. Even if Fran had needed it at the time, we still betrayed his trust.

I decided to apologize.

Yeah. Your armor was modified by Aristea, a blacksmith we met in Chrome. I'm sorry we did it without your permission...

"There's nothing to be sorry for! In fact, I'm honored!"

Wha? Uhh, does that mean you'll forgive us?

"There's nothing to forgive, my friends! I'd be a fool to get upset with the quality of that work of art you're wearing!" He inspected Fran's Black Sky Tiger set, looking genuinely touched. "They upgraded named items *so much*... Brilliant!"

It was done by a Godsmith, after all.

"Gah! If it wasn't for this whole mess, I'd love to become their apprentice..."

Really?

The finest blacksmith in Granzell becoming an apprentice? Well, I suppose it *would* mean learning from a legendary Godsmith. And it wasn't impossible either. Aristea should be in Belioth right now, but I wasn't sure if I should tell him that.

I'll mention you the next time that we meet her.

"You will?!" Garrus shouted, jumping out of bed. He grabbed Fran by the shoulders, forgetting that he was still recovering. "You'd really introduce me?"

Y-yeah. I don't know if they'll take you in though.

"I know that. I'll make do with a chance of being acquainted!"

We would tell Aristea about Garrus then. What happened after that would be up to her.

I should mention that they don't want to be used by people in power...

"I won't tell anyone about it!" Garrus said. "I promise!"

He wasn't one to go back on his word, but now he was looking at Fran like a predator eyeing his next meal. Was he really going to be all right?

"Can I have a closer look at your gear?" he asked.

"Hm."

The gear! Of course he was only interested in her gear! I should've known better.

He touched the fabric and knocked on its metallic parts. He looked like he was going to lean in to sniff it at one point, but he backed away. *Blacksmith joke*, he said. I was glad it was a joke, otherwise I would've needed to figure out a non-lethal way to punish the recovering dwarf. He inspected the detailing carefully.

"Hmm... Does Fran like this kind of look?"

No, Aristea just made it that way.

"I see...so this Godsmith is a woman?"

Yeah.

"I knew it. The armor looks exquisite. A woman's touch makes all the difference."

I thought that Garrus' iteration of Fran's armor was quite girly too. But apparently, he always tailored his work to his clients' preferences. Garrus' own taste was reflected in the Black Cat set's boyish look.

"Besides, the design changes are peanuts compared to the difference in strength. You don't see this kind of armor every day."

It's that good?

"That's right. Especially considering the base materials. Your average B-Rank doesn't have this kind of gear!"

Aristea's upgrade was more powerful and valuable than I'd thought.

"I can see that you're stronger too," Garrus said, looking at me.

Wait, really?

"*Significantly* stronger," Garrus muttered. "Even my Godsight can't see all the data now, but I can see that you're not the same sword I met in Alessa."

I appreciated the compliment, but it also made me nervous. Like having a professional appraiser tell you how much something is actually worth.

"Were you upgraded by Aristea, as well?" he asked.

Kind of, but there's more to it than that.

My circumstances weren't so easily to explain, and Garrus picked up on it immediately.

"Is that so... Well, I won't press you for the details. Just know that both of you have gotten *much* stronger."

You're making me blush.

This was the first time that anyone other than Fran had commented on my growth. Maybe I was just easy to please, but I felt genuinely happy.

Th-thanks...

"I should be thanking *you*," said Garrus. "I got to see the ultimate sword and an enhanced version of the armor I made. You've been a sight for sore eyes."

After that, we kept talking with Garrus about all sorts of things.

A few days after the incident...

I think it's time we left for Alessa.

"Hm."

Fran had finished her work and Garrus's fate was settled, so we no longer had any business in the capital. Still, I thought that Fran could do with a little more rest.

"I can finally train."

Fran, on the other hand, was raring to get going. I was also interested in what was happening up north. Had the Raydossian invasion been repelled? Was Alessa all right? Fran was interested too. Since their last communication, the north had been silent. More than that, Fran was very excited to train in the Demon Wolf's Garden. She couldn't help herself, really.

And so we decided to leave for Alessa. We needed to

drop by the guild there to get permission to enter the Garden. The Demon Wolf's Garden was an A-Rank haunt, and you needed to be at least B-Rank to enter. There wouldn't be any penalties if we entered without permission, but the guild could intervene. Besides, we might even be able to pick up some expedition quests while we were in town.

Not much left to do in the capital now that we have our reward.

"Hm."

But let's stop by the guild before we leave.

"Okay."

Fran had already received a bounty and some special rewards, but after issuing the reward for Garrus' safe-keeping, spending a lot of money at the auctions, and donating to the reconstruction of the local orphanage and shelter, we were now in the red. That being said, we still had five million gauld on hand, and all Fran's work meant that her approval rating skyrocketed.

She'd healed the wounded and donated to the poor, and people were beginning to call her the "Black Cat Saint." Fran preferred "Black Cat Princess" because it had a tougher ring to it, but the people of the capital mostly called her Saint. They even greeted her that way as she made her way to the guild, and I had a feeling that the nickname might even make it's to the neighboring towns and villages. Fran didn't seem pleased at this development, but I sure was.

Of course, Erianthe begged her to stay in the capital. After all, the Adventurer's Guild's ratings were through the roof with Fran was around.

"Stellia."

"Hey there. What brings you here today?" Stellia asked, lazily munching on a cookie.

The capital was finally settling back into a peaceful rhythm, and the senior receptionist could relax again.

"I need to talk to Erianthe."

"Come on in. She'll see you any time."

"Hm."

I guess Fran had an all-access pass at this point. It wasn't because of her rank promotion, but because of the trust she had built up here. Then again, it might've been because Stellia didn't want to go to Erianthe's office to tell her Fran was here.

There are people in Erianthe's office, I warned. *She might have visitors.*

"Hm."

Maybe we should visit another time. For now, we should just drop by to say hi and tell her we'd come back later.

Fran knocked on the door.

Ooh, that was a very good knock.

Hee hee.

Fran puffed out her chest slightly. It might not have seemed like anything remarkable, but to me, it was a greater mark of Fran's growth than her promotion. I mean for Fran to knock on a door before entering? That was astounding!

"Who is it? You can come in."

Whoever Erianthe's guests were, I guess they didn't need privacy. Fran entered the room and we found Erianthe chatting and laughing with some familiar fighters. It was the insectoid mercenaries we'd had the honor of fighting with, and the light atmosphere told me that they were good friends with her.

"Good timing. We were just talking about you." Erianthe said.

"About me?"

"Yes. These are my old friends. The mercenaries of Feeler and Shell."

"Hello there. I'm Robin. Sub-leader of Feeler and Shell."

The sharp lobster halfling held out his hand. Outside of combat, Robin looked mostly human—his patches of shell were gone, and the only signs of his insectoid blood where his feelers and black eyes. I had a feeling his everyday stats weren't as high as his combat stats either.

"The name's Hobbes."

"Effie..."

"Ann!"

"I am Shingen."

Grasshopper, mayfly, bull ant, and clam. All took turns introducing themselves.

Hobbes looked younger than Robin and had a cool air of smugness about him. Like his sub-leader, he looked quite human too. Effie the mayfly was quiet—even gloomy. Meanwhile, Ann the bull ant was brimming with energy. And, as expected, Shingen was as kind as he was strong.

"We usually operate in the small kingdoms down south," Robin said. "But we're up north on business. Lucky for us, we happened to be in the capital."

Fran tilted her head. "Lucky?"

Are you sure you don't mean unlucky? *You almost died a few days ago.*

"Yeah. We made it just in time to help our friend in need, after all."

"And make a little money on the side," Hobbes added.

Robin was as hot-blooded as he looked, but Hobbes adopted a more cynical outlook. Or at least, he tried to.

"It was a great fight..."

"We haven't gone all-out in a long time!"

Meanwhile, the two women enjoyed the heat of battle. They talked about the life-threatening fight as though it was the hottest piece of gossip. At least Robin wasn't one to visit death's door so readily. They seemed like Fran's kind of people, and it made me worry for her.

Shingen smiled casually. "I'm glad we all made it."

I could only imagine the pain he had to put up with. *Hang in there, my friend!*

"We won the battle thanks to you. And you seem to have helped Erianthe a great deal too. You have my gratitude."

"Robin!" Erianthe complained. "Stop talking like you're my dad!"

"How could I not thank her?" he said. "She saved our lives, and the life of our friend too."

"You're always so overbearing!" Erianthe said, exasperated.

But she didn't look all that bothered. She must've shared a deep bond with these mercenaries.

"A-anyway," Erianthe said, changing the subject. "You wanted to see me?"

Her face was beet red, but Fran didn't seem to notice.

"Hm. I'm going to Alessa."

"What? You're leaving the capital?"

"Hm."

"H-hang on!" Erianthe pleaded "There are so many things I wanted your help with!"

But Fran wasn't going to budge. Other adventurers could take care of the work, and the nobles were still buzzing around Fran. Eventually, Erianthe understood—nodding with a gloomy look on her face.

"Fine... When are you leaving?"

"Tomorrow."

"T-tomorrow? Can't it wait 'til next week?"

"Day after tomorrow?" Fran suggested.

"Longer! Can't you stay in the capital a while longer?"

Erianthe was probably calculating how many quests she could get Fran to do before she left. She was trying frantically to talk Fran into staying when Robin interrupted her.

"Now, now, Erianthe. You can't disrupt a warrior's journey like that."

Erianthe groaned. "You only say that because you're not stuck with my workload!"

"Actually, we were planning to stay here for a while to take on some work."

"R-really? Are you serious?"

"Yes."

"You're going to help me?"

"Yes."

"And that's a verbal agreement! You're stuck with me now! No getting away!"

Erianthe's friends smiled wryly at her pitiful excitement.

"You're the same as ever," Hobbes sighed.

"Really..."

"That's our Eri for you."

"That she is."

Oh, Erianthe... Poor Erianthe. Your competence is truly skin-deep.

Reincarnated as a sword

Epilogue

Hey...it's you again.

I wasn't asleep. I didn't *need* to sleep. But I was dreaming again. Still, this was becoming a semi-regular occurrence, and I was getting used to it. At the very least, there was no reason for me to panic while I was here. And by "here," I meant in the white void, with the same man in front of me—dressed in flowing robes with slicked-back silver hair.

Oh yeah, it's almost the Festival of the Moons again.

Usually, the capital would celebrate the festival, but current circumstances made that impossible. This year, there would just be a simple ritual. But apparently, this man drew strength from the Moons Festival—or rather, from the alignment of the moons. Because of that, I was expecting him to turn up.

Say, can you tell me who you are? I asked. *You're the unknown soul inside of me, aren't you? Are you Fenrir?*

Sorry. Can't tell you. Not yet.

I thought you said you'd tell me the next time we met?

Circumstances have changed...thanks to a certain someone. I can't tell you who I am right now. It might be dangerous. The memories could...

What do you mean? I asked.

I need you to trust me on this one.

All right...

The man's serious tone was enough to convince me that things were dire.

You look worn out, I told him.

He looked a little different than he had before. His dignified and driven aura was gone, now replaced with a haggard look. He was pale, and there were bags under his eyes. His cheeks looked sunken too.

Stuff happened. And there have been anomalies with you too.

What?

You may know this already, but you are in slight—er, grave danger.

Are you talking about that strange voice?

The voice had demanded things. "Devour everything!

EPILOGUE

Heaven and earth, gods and demons, man and beast, everything!"

At least, that's if I remembered it correctly. The voice was brutal. That was all I needed to know.

That's not the only thing, said the man.

There's more?

Much, much more. But I don't have the power to solve those problems here.

No wonder he went out of his way to appear before me.

In any case, here's what you need to do. Come to the Demon Wolf's Garden within twenty days.

Twenty days? I asked. *Should I go to the altar?*

That's right. The Lunar mana should still be at its peak then.

Lunar mana. First, he got stronger during the Moons Festival, and now this. I was beginning to wonder if he was a servant of the Goddess of the Silver Moon. The man was a man, after all, so he couldn't be the goddess herself.

I'll tell you who I am when you're there, among other things.

Wait—

And then he was gone, taking the white void along with him. My vision cleared, and I was left staring at our inn room. I guess he only needed my mind to talk with me in the white void.

Dammit! He always does all the talking!

At least I got critical information out of him this time.

The altar in the Demon Wolf's Garden.

The place where I first awakened in this world. Apparently it held other secrets too. We were already going to the Garden so Fran could train, but now we had another reason to go.

"Teacher...?"

Sorry, Fran. Did I wake you?

"Hm... I felt something weird."

Actually—

I told her about what just happened. Fran already knew about the strange voice that came up after I Cannibalized Fanatix, and it made her worry. I tried to reassure her by saying that I was the same as I'd always been.

"We have to get to the Garden!"

Of course she'd want to leave right away. We were going to see the head court doctor today, but I was worried she might want to skip that appointment.

Calm down, we still have twenty days. We can take a few days to get to Alessa, and the Garden itself isn't that large. No need to rush.

"But he said you're in danger."

EPILOGUE

Sure, but he didn't sound desperate, and he gave us a twenty-day head start, so we don't need to be there this instant.

We needed to hurry, sure, but we didn't need to rush.

Besides, we should meet with the bigwigs before we leave for Alessa.

"Okay..."

Fran understood the need for etiquette—at least, I hoped she did. I didn't think she would skip her lunch appointment with the court doctors so readily. When we got there, the head court doctor and chamberlain complimented her fine work, but she ignored most of their comments.

The luncheon took around thirty minutes, and I never thought I'd see the day Fran wouldn't finish her plate... but she excused herself early by saying, "I have to go to Alessa." Everyone paused for a moment, but they were strangely willing to let her go. They must have thought that she needed to leave at once—perhaps because she'd accepted a quest. Something to do with preparing for the Raydossian invasion. Either way, I was willing to let the misunderstanding stand, especially since no one gave her any flack for it.

"Teacher, let's go to Alessa!"

All right, all right.

There was no stopping her now.

"Do your best, Jet."

"Woof!"

Jet should get there in four days without any trouble. Fran got on his back, but before we could leave, someone called out to her.

"Fran! Wait!"

"Erianthe?"

"I can't believe you would just leave without saying goodbye! Good thing I posted lookouts near the gates!"

Erianthe was prepared for Fran's departure and ordered the guild to keep an eye out for her. Besides, it wasn't like we could leave right away. We still needed to line up at the gates for departure. Now, Erianthe, Colbert, Garrus, and Count Bayreeds were here to see Fran off.

"Do you need something?" Fran said.

"Look," Erianthe sighed. "Oh, never mind."

I sympathized with her exasperation.

"We're here to thank you before you go," she said, bowing her head deeply. "You did a lot to help the capital. And, as the representative of all the adventurers here, thank you."

The others came to shake Fran's hand and bow in respect, and applause started breaking out everywhere. The guards watching the gates, the adventurers who'd just entered the city, and the citizens around us all joined in. The clapping got louder and louder until it became a thundering applause. It was easy to imagine the sound reverberating through the city—you could probably even hear it from the castle.

"Thank you so much for saving us, Saint Fran!"

"Come visit us again soon!"

"Thank you, Saint Fran!"

This was probably the first time so many people had gathered to wish us well, and Fran's eyes widened with surprise. To her, she only defeated her enemy and did what she could to help. She knew that the people she'd helped would want to thank her, but she didn't understand why everyone else was involved.

"Why?" she asked.

"Because you did something amazing! Get with the program already!"

She's right, Fran. You helped far more people than you imagined.

Hm...

Fran was still bothered by the fact that she slept through the Fanatix fight and didn't think what she'd done was that significant.

Try waving your hand, Fran.

"My hand?"

Fran raised her hand, and it was greeted with even louder cheers.

Everyone raised their voices to thank her.

This is how they feel about what you've done, Fran. They're all really grateful. You should feel proud.

"Hm..."

"Come again soon, Fran! We'll welcome you anytime!"

"Come show me your gear again!"

"Thank you!"

Fran took in the blessings and words of encouragement, and then told Jet to run. She was blushing. She tried to hide it, but I could tell. The ghost of a smile formed on her lips.

The capital's been through a lot...I hope they recover soon.

"Hm."

Next stop, good old Alessa.

"Can't wait."

"Woof!"

Still, it had only been six months since we were last there.

"Come on, Jet! Full speed ahead!"

"Arf! Woof woof!"

Aaah, you don't have to go so fast!

"We'll be fine!"

"Woof!"

This is not fiiiiiine!

Reincarnated as a sword

Let your imagination take flight with Seven Seas' light novel imprint: Airship

Discover your next great read at
www.airshipnovels.com

Experience all that SEVEN SEAS has to offer!

SEVENSEASENTERTAINMENT.COM
Visit and follow us on Twitter at twitter.com/gomanga/